HARRY BONE-THIEF

HARRY BONE-THIEF

JAN SHIRLEY

Ragged Bears Publishing

RAGGED BEARS
Published by Ragged Bears Publishing Ltd.
Unit 14A, Bennetts Field Industrial Estate,
Southgate Road,
Wincanton,
Somerset BA9 9DT, UK

First published 2011
1 3 5 7 9 10 8 6 4 2

A CIP catalogue record for this book is available from the British
Library

ISBN 978 1 85714 449 9
Printed in Poland

CONTENTS

Acknowledgments

The Author would like to thank the following who helped her create *Harry Bone-Thief*:

Mick, who showed me how to use an adze, Janni who made me rewrite this book not once but twice, and Douglas who took the trouble to tell me he liked it.

I am also most grateful to the staff in the Visits Office at Canterbury Cathedral and to Stephen Bax, whose website www.canterburybuildings.com is a joy. Readers who want to know where Harry Wright and his family lived can look at Stephen's site, click on one of the beautiful maps, walk in through the West Gate and turn left into St Peter's Lane, close by the River Stour. It was somewhere along there.

People in the Story –

HARRY WRIGHT, younger son of:
THOMAS WRIGHT, master carpenter
PETER, Harry's older brother
ELLIE, his older sister
LUCY, his baby sister
CLARE is Thomas's second wife, mother of Harry and Lucy
GREAT AUNT ROSE, a grumpy old lady
PEGGY ANN, helps in the house
LIPPERTY JACK, a lost child
FATHER BENEDICT, parish priest
JOSHUA, a cathedral monk, Clare's brother
BROTHER BERNARD, a senior monk
BROTHER SIMON, a junior monk,
and they all obey FATHER PRIOR
WILL, PAUL, JOHNNY, cathedral workmen
SAINT THOMAS BECKET, a difficult archbishop,
    dead
HENRY VIII, a dangerous king
MASTER SECRETARY CROMWELL
Also ARCHBISHOP CRANMER, SCULLY, a greasy
    boy, French lords and ladies, JOE and COBBY, horses

CHAPTER ONE
DANGER

I still wake suddenly sometimes, sweat streaming off me, and remember. Then I come properly awake and remind myself that this is now, it's all right. All right. Safe.

Yes, it was dangerous, that hot summer of 1538 here in Canterbury, but I was young, ridiculously young. I had no idea at all.

My father smashed and bloody, unrecognisable, how could I know?

I remember sitting under the kitchen table and people were talking, just the usual mutter. Why would I listen? I was miles away inside my head, sailing a warship across towards France. I would find those Frenchmen, blow them out of the water, drown them. She was a three-master, I remember that, and I had to make sure we were all at our posts, wide awake, the sheets taut, sails pulling, guns ready. We were running before a fair wind, white horses dancing, and the ship lifted and smacked down again, lifted and smacked. I eased my grip on the tiller and kept her close on her course.

Then I caught sight of my sister Ellie's bare feet dangling close by my nose and there was a brown hen's feather lying on the floor near my hand. I picked it up and was just going to draw it across the sole of her foot when I heard a shout. My older brother Peter, yelling – and that wasn't like him –

'Father, no!' Then nothing. Then Peter again – 'How can you even think of it? The danger! All of us. Even little Lucy. You will die, and so shall I, the king will have us both hanged, and Clare and the young ones will starve. No one to work for them, no food. Do you *want* them to die of hunger?'

Hanged? Die of hunger? What would my father say? No, all I heard was my uncle, Brother Joshua from the Priory, really angry. We saw quite a lot of him in those days because he was a monk in the Priory just nearby. Sang in the cathedral. Father calls him an excitable soul, and so he is, but all the same he's a good friend. Usually. At that moment he was furious. He and Peter are the same sort of age, nineteen or so that summer, and they never agreed about anything. They still don't. One wants the new religion from Germany, the other would fight to hell and back for the old one in Rome. Everything in English, no pope, never mind about the saints, that's Peter. Everything in Latin, the pope can't be wrong, the blessed saints talk to God for you, that's Uncle Joshua.

Now Joshua was blazing at Peter, telling him what a fool he was.

'Can't you see it?' he said. 'The king's men are coming! King Harry's men! We've no time, they're on their way, you know they are, and your father will help, he must! We've got to *save the Saint!*'

Well, I'd heard enough, that was nonsense. Everyone knew that Saint Thomas was the one who did the saving, he didn't need it. He was up there in heaven, great and glorious, could go anywhere, do anything. You had a broken leg? Ask the Saint. A bad fever? Ask the Saint. Your aunt has gone mad? Ask the Saint. Pigs and chickens and cattle too. Cats? Don't know, maybe. But what rubbish Uncle Josh was talking, 'save the Saint' indeed! I stopped listening and drew the brown feather across the sole of Ellie's foot. She yelled and jumped up.

Nothing much was broken. Peggy Ann pretended to clip me round the head, but she didn't mean it. She mopped up the spills and began clearing the dishes away. Peter went off tight-lipped into the workshop and Father took Uncle Josh into the garden and walked him to and fro.

'I work in the Saint's cathedral,' I heard him telling Josh. 'Have done all my life. I'll help. I'm not going to let him down now.'

Mother put one arm round me and the other round Ellie and told us to be friends. We are really. Ellie is only my half-sister, she's three years older than me and thinks she knows best about everything but she's all right. Her own mother died when Ellie was born, but then my mum came along, Clare, and you'd never know she and Ellie weren't related. They even look a bit like each other, curly fair hair and cheerful faces. So there's Peter, dark and tall like Father, and next there's Ellie, and then there's me, Harry, and baby Lucy, and everyone loves Lucy, even Aunt Rose.

Aunt Rose, really she's Great Aunt Rose, sits by the fire and grumbles. She's never happy unless she's miserable. There she sat now moaning away:

'If God had not taken my Priscilla, she would have known how to keep this family in order! A sad loss!' But we'd long ago stopped taking any notice of old mumble grumble.

I heard Dad coming in from the garden and scooted into the workshop. Peter was planing down a length of beech wood. He didn't stop what he was doing but nodded towards a heap of short split pieces of oak that needed their corners rasping off, ready to be shaped into pegs. I got on with them.

Father came in and picked up the adze. A good heavy thing, that is, does all the work by its own weight, I love using it, when I'm allowed. There he stood letting its sharp head swing to and fro by his feet, shaping an elm plank that was going to be part of a coffin, but he didn't say anything. Nor did Peter.

I rasped away at the pegs. No one has ever managed to persuade Father to change his mind, you might as well argue with an oak tree. I began working the *Great Harry* out of Rye harbour, warping her out against a foul wind, but oh no, Peter began again.

'Father, don't you remember? Barton, Bocking, Dereham, good men and women, people we knew, *dead*. Like the Chancellor, God help him!'

I knew about the Chancellor, and shivered. He'd been a great man, Master More, and I often see his daughter, she lives just down the road from us. King Harry had him killed, his head cut off, because he wouldn't give in. He just would not agree that the king, not the pope, was the right person to rule the Church in England. A king can't rule a Church, he said, only a pope. This king can, does! said King Harry. No! said the Chancellor, he doesn't, can't ... And so, chop. And they'd been friends, *friends*, those two men. Brrr! And that brave lady managed to get her father's poor dead head down off its spike above London Bridge and bring it home to Canterbury. She can't have climbed up there herself, she must have paid someone to do it for her. Brave him too.

Now Josh wanted my dad to annoy this king? I hoped not.

So did Peter. He was still in full blast – 'And those poor fools in the North, so stupid! believed the king when he said oh yes, of course he'd forgive them – come along, come along, everything's all right! And along they come and whee! up they go – onto the gallows, hanged, slashed open still alive, their guts heaved out – for God's sake, Father, *think*, kings are dangerous!'

Father stepped off the board he was working on, turned it over and stepped back onto it to trim the other side. My big brother tried again:

'This king, listen! *tigers* are safer! Mess with Harry and you're dead. We *know* that, we've seen it! And a few old bones, how can they matter? Miracles, magic, rubbishy old trash, let them burn! Listen to Luther, he knows, he's the one we should trust. Poor silly Joshua, if only he'd grow up, but he's so *stupid!* Let the king's men take Becket's rotten old bones away, good riddance!'

'Luther? Martin Luther?' said my father. 'Didn't King Harry say he was a wolf from hell?' He stood up straight and stretched. 'And a poisonous viper, wasn't it? But never mind him – what matters is that it's no way to treat our Saint, throwing him out onto a dung-heap. He's looked after us here in Canterbury for hundreds of years. Healed us, protected us, spoken up for us in heaven. And us Wrights, we've worked for him always and I'm not stopping now. What I am doing,' he added, 'if people will let me, is getting this coffin finished and ready for poor old Jim Brand's funeral before we have to take time off and go down to Rye.'

I liked going down to Rye – Grandfather Stephens, the harbour, boats – I wanted to ask why, but on rolled brother Peter, intent on the battle.

'They'll rack you to pieces and burn you dead and you can go and sit in heaven and polish your damned halo!' he cried , 'but it won't be just you, it will be all of us!'

'Oh no,' said my father. 'I'll manage better than that. Get on with that length of beech, it's nowhere near smooth.'

More silence.

The door to the kitchen was open, and I could hear my mother and Ellie talking. Mother was remembering King Harry from way back.

'I saw him, you know, before he began to hate Saint Thomas, when he came here to pray at the Saint's shrine. What a different world it was! He was still married to Queen Catherine, of course, and he brought her nephew with him, the emperor, and I saw both of them quite close. I was only little, about ten, and I thought I'd never get to the front of the crowd, but then people noticed how small I was and let me through. And there he was, all golden and glowing and smiling! So tall too. I thought he was wonderful.'

'Why does he hate our Saint?' I asked.

'Oh, are you there, Harry? I thought you were working!'

'Well yes, so I am!' I ran my fingers over the oak pegs, checking for rough places. Some needed a bit more work, and I went on rubbing them down. 'But why does King Harry hate the Saint?'

'Because he's the king,' Great Aunt Rose called through from her corner by the fire. 'Because he wants to go on shutting down the monasteries and helping himself to their money. Very rich, those monks! And because our Saint Thomas stood up to another King Henry all those hundreds of years ago, stood up for Holy Church, stood up for Canterbury! Died for Canterbury.'

'That King Harry killed him?' I asked, not being quite sure.

'Yes, had him killed, and then later on he had to come here and say he never meant it to happen and how sorry he was and let the Prior and all the monks take turns beating him. Wearing just his shirt and drawers.'

'Beating the *king*?' I said. 'No one beats kings!'

'Eighty monks, three whacks each,' Peter chipped in, looking up from the length of beech wood. 'Maybe they didn't hit very hard, I don't know.'

That was amazing. I shook my head, tipped the pegs

into their box, looked around for the broom and began to sweep up.

Through in the kitchen I heard Ellie ask,

'What's an emperor exactly?' and Mother answered,

'Oh, someone even grander than a king. That one was Charles, Emperor of Germany. He was here visiting his aunt, our Queen Catherine I mean, poor lady. But I don't really remember him. Only King Harry.'

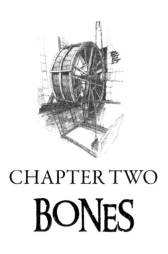

CHAPTER TWO
BONES

It was next day, almost dinner time. Good smells in the big sunny kitchen. Great Aunt Rose sitting up and looking ready. Cat on windowsill watching birds.

'There now!' said my mother. 'If your father and Peter haven't gone off without their dinners. And Peggy Ann has enough to do.' She wrapped this and that in a cloth, put it into a basket and handed it to Ellie. 'Here you are, love, take them this, will you? They're working in the wheel loft.' Ellie nodded and darted off. She's a quick girl, my sister. But I'm quick too, and I like the wheel loft and I'm never allowed there on my own – some nonsense about danger, and me being too young – and I darted after her and soon caught her up.

We trotted through the lanes and under the great archway and along to the Cathedral. It wasn't far. There it stood, always new, always having bits added on, and I glanced quickly up at the great tall tower – my tower! – as we went in. I'm Harry and it's Harry too, the Bell Harry Tower. We Wrights helped build it. It got its name because Bell Harry sits on the very top of the tower, out in the open, my bell! and it makes a good strong sound. Calls the monks to prayer, tells you when people die, how old they were, all sorts of things. Anyway, there we were and in we went, in through the little door to the tower steps, and up and up and up. And round and round. Stone, twisty, noisy, clattering.

And then up some more. It's certainly a very high tower. We were only going part way up, but even so ...

At last we were there. Ellie stopped to get her breath but I ran past her onto the wide open space, the wheel loft. It's where the treadmill stands, a huge wheel, and it takes three men to work it. They get inside it and walk and walk, and so it keeps turning round and powers a pulley so that we can lift stone and timber up from the floor of the Cathedral miles below. All this stuff gets hauled up and the crane lifts it in through a big opening in the loft floor. But the trapdoor was closed and locked and the wheel was standing still. I liked seeing it working.

I ran to it all the same and was just climbing inside when of course I heard my father's voice, 'None of that, boy! Stay clear!' So I did.

Father took the basket from Ellie and asked her why

ever she'd brought me, and she laughed and said, 'No one brings Harry, he just comes.'

'So he does,' said my dad. 'Harry, sit down and stay in one place!'

I curled up close to Peter and looked hopefully at his cold sausage. Cheese and pickle as well. Johnny and Paul were there too, and Will, they work with Dad in the cathedral, of course they'd brought their own dinners.

'Yours is waiting for you at home,' said my tall brother, but I told him I would die of hunger before I got back. He smiled and gave me half a sausage. Johnny gave me a bit of his onion, and I crunched that, then thought I would explore a bit. I love it up there, it is so amazing to be on top, *on top* of a ceiling, and to think that you've got the whole great emptiness of the cathedral there underneath you. And somehow it feels like a ship with all those huge timbers rising away into the darkness and holding up the massive roof. There are decked walkways leading off in different directions, and I slid away from beside Peter and began to look into the interesting spaces underneath one of these.

Not for long. I heard Father telling the others to move.

'Come on, we need those new timbers up here. Get the hatch uncovered, set up the crane and stand by to work the wheel. Paul, Johnny, you go down and handle the stuff there, we three will work the wheel. Ellie, you and Harry go on down, can't have you up here while we're working.' So I crawled out, rather dusty, and Ellie grabbed me – no need for that! – and marched me off to the stair doorway. Down and down and down, you could easily get giddy twirling round those stairs. Down at the bottom and out through the door, and we stopped to look up at where we'd been. That huge round hatchway, from here it looked like a bit of a dot, a nothing.

'Small as mice, we are,' I said to Ellie. 'If you look down, I mean.'

'From up there? Yes, but come on, I'm hungry. And there's Father whistling orders down to Paul and Johnny, and all these timbers to shift, we'll be in the way.'

Home and dinner. Peter says I eat like a starving cormorant, but what does he know about it? I'm the one that knows about the sea and sea birds.

'Quite tasty,' I heard Great Aunt Rose say in a grudging voice. 'Needs more salt. You're a goodish cook, Clare, but you'll never come near my Priscilla. If those two young gannets don't want it, I'll have that last bit of onion pie.' Cormorants, gannets, I don't know. What did she think she was? I was still hungry, and flashed a glance at Mother. She was sitting nursing baby Lucy, but she smiled at me, then got up and slid the last piece of pie onto the old vulture's plate. Then she picked up a covered dish from the side of the fire, took off its lid and gave me a good helping of sausage and beans.

Next came a knock at the door and in came Uncle Joshua, Mother's young brother. She smiled and offered him some left over dinner but he said no thanks, he'd eaten.

'I mustn't stop,' he said. 'We're learning a new chant, quite tricky, have to get back. The only thing is, I do need a quick word with Thomas about ... er ... um, about ...'

'About those bones?' said my mother. 'Here, have some sausage and cheer up. Leave it to Thomas. If he says he'll do it, then he will. You ought to know that by now.'

'Bones?' said my silly young uncle in horror. 'Clare, don't say it! I promised! You don't know anything about it, no one does! I *promised!*'

I saw Great Aunt Rose collecting up the last little bits of pie on her plate and putting them in her mouth.

'Everybody knows everything,' she said through a shower of crumbs. 'You were going on and on at Peter about it only yesterday, remember?'

Uncle Joshua gulped, nodded, muttered something about getting back, and vanished.

'Why do bones matter?' I asked Mother. I knew they did, but didn't know why. She was collecting plates and dishes together from the table, but now she stopped and thought.

'It's the Resurrection, isn't it?' she said. 'Yes, that's right. On Judgement Day, when Christ comes in glory and the world ends, and the dead wake up. We all rise up

24

out of our graves and come before the great Judge and he sorts us out into sheep and goats. Good and bad.'

'And the good ones go to sit beside him in heaven for ever and ever and the bad ones are dragged off to hell and the everlasting fire,' said Great Aunt Rose cheerfully. 'And if you haven't got your bones, you can't rise up. You be sure and bury me carefully when my time comes.'

'Deep as deep,' said Mother, laughing. 'Don't you worry!'

'What about drowned sailors?' I asked.

'Oh they'll come dancing up, whales and sharks and whatnot all spitting them out,' said my mother. 'What a sight it will be!'

'Smelly,' I said. 'Stinking! Hundreds of years some of them, rotting away, all foul and fishy.'

'No no,' said Mother. 'Just nice clean shiny bones.'

So that was all right.

She gathered the dishes together and took them away into the scullery, and I went off into the workshop. Fresh cut shavings and new sawdust, it's always a good smell in there. Peter set me to dressing the ends of the elm planks Father had been working on.

I wondered why King Harry wanted to dig Saint Thomas up. Helping himself to all the jewels and treasure and amazing things on the shrine, yes, I could understand that, but what good were the bones going to do him? Why did he want them?

'He doesn't,' said Peter when I asked him. 'He'll have them burnt. Quite right too. All that silly mumbo jumbo about bits of dead bone working miracles, well, that's nonsense, that's got to go.'

It had, had it? I knew what my uncle Joshua would say about that, but didn't bother getting into an argument.

with fear. Not dumb, because he did speak once, told me his name. Lipperty Jack, that's who he was, he said so, but that was all he did say. 'Lipperty Jack,' once, and then nothing more. I told him I was Harry Wright, I chattered on about Rye and Canterbury and riding here on Cobby and – oh, it was all getting nowhere, and he just seemed to shrink, get smaller and smaller and still kept shivering.

This needed more than I could do, and I took hold of his hand and climbed back up the hill and found my family. He seemed quite willing to come.

They were beginning to wonder where I was, and thinking about harnessing Cobby and setting off for home. I told them how I'd found him.

'He can't be more than three!' said my mother looking at the tiny boy in amazement. 'Four at most! But who does he belong to?'

'Me!' I said firmly. 'Me.'

They asked all over Rye but no one seemed to know anything useful.

'Seen him around for a while now,' said one man. 'Just a beggar, too many of them, can't think why the law doesn't move them on.'

A woman, not quite so nasty, said she'd tried to make friends with the child but ... 'He just runs off and hides. Won't speak, won't anything. A waste of time really.'

Lipperty held tight to my hand and never said a word.

A waste of time, so it was, people like that. So we harnessed up, put Cobby between the shafts and Mother and Aunt Rose climbed on board. I lifted Lippy up and put him in the cart – couldn't tell whether he felt safe there or not, but he settled close to Mother and baby Lucy and stayed still. Father rode big black cart-horsey Joe, and Peter was on a hired mare, Moonlight. Ellie and I took turns riding Cobby or in the cart and often just jumped out and ran. Reaching the cliffs below Lymne, we went the long way round by Dymchurch for the horses' sake, but even so everyone got out and walked, even Aunt Rose. And Lippy.

CHAPTER FOUR
GREAT GRANDFATHER

How was my dad going to save Saint Thomas's bones? No use asking, he would just smile and say nothing. I did try telling him I could help, I was small and could get into difficult places, like between the bars that made a fence all round the Saint's tomb, but really I knew it, he only laughed and shook his head.

It was pure chance that sent me looking for Lipperty in our own parish church a few mornings later. Strange tiny creature, he'd settled in with us well as far as we could see – ate, slept, ran about and all that, although he still never spoke. And he kept close to me, hardly let me out of his sight. So that when one morning he didn't seem to be anywhere around, I wondered if I ought to be worried. Perhaps he was just getting braver and was perfectly all right somewhere or other.

We'd had breakfast, Father had gone off to do

some repairs somewhere, whistling cheerfully, and I should have been in the workshop doing odd jobs and sweeping up sawdust. Peter was out with Johnny and the others working in the Cathedral. But I wanted to check on Lipperty.

Bell Harry sounded just as I was running out of the house, so I knew it was still quite early. It rings four times a day, my bell does, to call the monks to prayer. Well, it did then. No monks now. I ran up the High Street a bit – no Lipperty – ran down it the other way – no Lipperty – thought, Oh this is silly, I'll go home, but then, no, here's Saint Peter's, why not turn in and look there?

Now that was odd, I thought, standing just inside the main door. No Lipperty, but never mind that, what was my father doing over there by Great Grandfather's grave?

I wasn't meaning to spy on him, but I was so surprised I just stood and watched as he levered up the big flagstone over the grave in the north aisle. I knew what it said on it, of course I did:

Here lies the body of Harry Wright
Master Carpenter
fell and died in the Cathedral Church of Christ
in the year of grace 1476
in his 43rd year
You that pass by, pray for his soul

What was Father doing? Digging him up?

He got the flagstone shifted aside, then knelt down and set to work getting the coffin lid off. That wasn't easy, but after a bit it came loose and he lifted it away and began to take handfuls of bones out of the coffin. I couldn't stay still any longer but ran forward and said,

'What is it, Dad, can I help?'

What a shock I gave him. Hadn't meant to do that.

His jaw dropped open and he went all white, dreadful.

Then he shut his mouth again, took a deep breath, and said, 'Harry, why aren't you in the workshop?'

'You look nearly as dead as Great Grandfather,' I said. 'What's the matter? I didn't mean to surprise you.'

The colour began to come back into his face and he laughed.

'I thought I'd use his bones,' he said. 'Some of them. But no, I won't risk it. Think of another plan.'

'I was really looking for Lipperty,' I said. 'Have you seen him?'

'No. But he won't be far. Here, help me pack your Great Grandfather up again.' He handed me a couple of long bones and I leaned forward to put them in the coffin – I don't mind coffins, don't mind bones, Father's a carpenter and an undertaker, he's always made coffins for people and I'm absolutely used to them – but I stopped with the leg bones in my hand and said, 'You don't have to change your mind. You can trust me not to tell. Is it to do with the Saint?'

My poor father, his jaw dropped again! But this time he shut it up fast, said, 'Go home *now*, and sweep up the workshop floor,' and added, 'and that's an order.' Yes, all right, I was on my way.

I ran home, and there in the kitchen was a fine hot yeasty smell and Lipperty kneeling up on a stool and watching my mother and Ellie make bread. Mother was shaping plain loaves and Ellie was twisting a complicated plait.

'Where *were* you?' I said to Lippy, but of course I just got a smile, and then I begged a bit of dough from Mother, pulled it into two halves and gave one bit to Lipperty. I settled down to make a little merchant vessel, heavily laden, deep in the water, and as far as I could see Lippy was making a horse. Probably a horse. It was rolling on its back but he was having problems with the legs.

Then I heard footsteps and I flew into the workshop and seized the broom.

The bread was ready, dinner was ready, and Mother had remembered to bake the little ship and the rolling horse. I sailed my boat in and out among the plates and dishes till Mother told me for goodness' sake to stop it. Lippy put his lumpy little horse down in front of his place at table and gazed lovingly at it. Then suddenly he scrambled down off his stool, picked it up and went and gave it to Mother. He did it very carefully, with a low bow, as if it really really mattered, and Mother kissed him and very nearly burst into tears.

'A well-born baby, that,' said Great Aunt in her usual sour voice. 'Some fine lady somewhere should have looked after him better.'

CHAPTER FIVE
GET OUT THOSE BONES

I was worried about the danger. Other things too. Of course I could see what Dad had been planning to do – he was going to take Saint Thomas's bones out of the shrine and put Great Grandfather's there instead. Squirrel the rescued bones away somewhere safe inside the Cathedral. Then Great Grandfather would get burnt up and not the Saint.

Wouldn't he mind?

What about the Resurrection and all the bones rising up, buried in the earth or drowned in the sea? Where would Great Grandfather be then?

But then Peter could be right, once you've finished using your body, it's done with, just dead meat, goodbye. Your soul, the real you, is in heaven with the angels – or in hell with the devils of course – and that's that.

But our Saint has lain here in his own cathedral all

these hundreds of years and belongs here with us and he doesn't want to be thrown out. Treated like rubbish.

So I was confused. Then I decided that I ought to stop bothering and Saint Thomas was quite capable of making things right for Great Grandfather. Leave it to him.

I remembered Mother taking Ellie and me to visit the shrine, the Saint's tomb, one day last summer, and all the jewels blazing and all the people praying. I think it was Ellie's birthday. Not long before Lucy was born. Mother hung a little gold and pearl cross there among all the other things people had given when they wanted help for something, and she prayed to Saint Thomas for a safe delivery and a healthy baby. Our Saint, and he cares about us.

I remembered another time when I was quite small myself and I'd wanted to touch one of the treasures hanging on the shrine and Brother Bernard, who is tall, thin and fierce, smacked my hand away and gave me a telling off. I hadn't been going to hurt it – it was an old old walrus tusk, once belonged to an Icelandic chieftain, people said, and I used to think of him in his furs bobbing about in a little boat among all those ice floes and seals and things. What could have brought him to Canterbury? To pray to the Saint for something, I suppose, or just on his way somewhere else, perhaps to the Holy Land, to fight the heathen for Christ. Hot sun and the blazing light shining on polished steel, heavy horses struggling over the loose sand, pennons fluttering as the knights lowered their lances for the charge. Poor man, he wouldn't like it much, not after snow and ice and white bears. Perhaps he would be glad to be suffering for Jesus' sake.

And now King Harry would have that little cross and the walrus tusk and everything else, all that treasure. How could he possibly need it? And how soon were his men coming?

I wished I knew.

Next morning I happened to wake early, very early. It was only beginning to be light, just a kind of grey half-light, and look, there was my father up and dressed and treading very quietly downstairs. I lay and listened. Into the workshop. Collecting tools. The beginning of a clatter, quickly checked.

I looked round. No one else was awake. Softly, not disturbing anyone, I slid away from my sleeping brother, picked up a handful of clothes, crept halfway down the steps – there was my father, going out of the workshop door and carrying a short ladder. And a sack.

So early? Alone?

I jumped into my clothes and followed him.

Quietly, gently, keeping well back, all through the lanes, into the Precincts, over to the Cathedral's side door, in and up the Pilgrims' Steps.

Now to the tomb? It was never left unguarded. Yes, I could see Brother Simon on duty, a real friend, and Brother Joshua, my uncle. Of course, who else? Father would have seen to that.

I was small and good at keeping still. They never noticed me.

The tall pillars I've known all my life rose upwards into the dim early light, good hiding places, and I stole from pillar to pillar, from tomb to tomb, and crept up close. I could see Saint Thomas all round me – there behind me in the half light were the great windows full of pictures, the Saint healing a leper, the Saint healing a mad woman, the Saint, the Saint, all the many stories of the good he had done since he died, his miracles of help and healing, our Saint. And there in front of me stood his tomb, his shrine, holy and ancient, where Saint Thomas had lain for so many hundreds of years, and now my father was breaking into it.

I wondered if he was frightened. If he was, he wouldn't let it matter.

The wooden cover was down over the tomb, no glitter, no glory, but Simon nodded to my father and flung a couple of rugs over the whole thing so as to stop the little guard bells jingling – they sang and jangled when the cover was moved, but not this time – and then he and Uncle Josh heaved on the rope. Up came the cover, up and up – but I was puzzled, Father wasn't helping them, he had turned away and was setting up his ladder against another tomb, a different one. Why there? Never mind the Black Prince, get on with the job. Rescue the Saint!

Then I understood. If anyone did come by, Brother Bernard or someone – heaven forbid, not him! – they would think Father was working on the Prince's tomb, not the Saint's. A decoy. Clever.

Then he got going on the real job. Simon and Joshua stood each of them some distance away to keep watch. First he unfastened the lock on the end section of the iron rails that went right round the shrine, then began using a hammer and chisel to peck at the mortar holding the stonework together at the foot of the tomb itself. He had a cloth over the handle of the chisel to muffle it but even so it made quite a noise. Now and then he stopped and glanced up towards the watchers, but they nodded towards him to go on, and he did.

No one would see me if I moved carefully. There are railings round the Black Prince and there's a big flat canopy hanging over his tomb. There he lies underneath it, golden and glittering, son of a king. Black at heart, cruel, a great fighter. Defeated those French time and again.

I would be able to see much better if I was on top of that canopy looking down. If I picked the right moment – I waited till Joshua had walked right out of sight down the south aisle to keep guard in that direction and Simon was a good distance off in the Corona, and swarmed quietly up the ladder. No chance of Father seeing me, he was head down and battling with the stonework of the tomb.

I lay there flat, just my head sticking out over the edge. How different it all looked from up here! Interesting. Those windows too, beginning to blaze now as the early sunshine poured through them, blues, greens and reds, the Saint all colourful and glowing, helping people, healing them, telling them off, wonderful. Couldn't he save his own bones? Yes, perhaps he was doing exactly that, using us.

The light threw bars and patches of colour onto the stone floor, and I watched them move and shift as the time ran on.

Full daylight now, hurry up.

By now Father had all the bits of stonework out and separate, laid to one side in careful order. You could see the whole end of the actual coffin. It was huge, very heavy, with a small dusty window at this end for people to peer through at a pair of dead feet. Father stood up, beckoned to Simon and together slowly, carefully, they managed to ease this great bulky chest out onto the floor. It scraped, they couldn't help it, too much noise. But no one came.

Then footsteps.

In a flash Father was up his ladder by the Black Prince, tapping thoughtfully at the underside of the canopy. I lay on top of it, shrunk as small as small, and listened.

Oh, it was Ellie! Ellie and little Lipperty.

CHAPTER SIX
HIDE THEM, HIDE THEM

'Simon, Joshua, take them away! Take them home!'
Father's voice. But Simon said, no, they were on duty,
couldn't go, and 'anyway you need us to keep watch.'
I heard Ellie saying they wouldn't be in the way, 'and
we'll help you keep watch.' Carefully I slid forward,
caught Ellie's eye and waved at her, then put my finger
to my lips. Her face changed from astonishment to a
huge smile, and I saw her touch Lippy's cheek and turn
his face towards me. A good thing he never talked!
He smiled like a sunrise, then closed his lips tight and
turned away towards Father and the others.

Father was kneeling at the side of the Saint's coffin,
getting the lid free. As I watched he raised it slowly up,
eased it back – and stopped, frozen.

Why?

I saw too.

There was a face there. Bleak, long, severe, eyes closed. For a dreadful moment I thought they would open, the dead man would blaze out, ask how we dared touch him, but then it changed, crumbled, vanished. Now all I could see were a few bones, the remains of a skull, some teeth.

And something glittering – a shining cup?

My poor father was just as horrified as I was, I could see that. He knelt there stone still, then at last shook himself, drew a deep breath and stood up.

If shocks could kill, he'd have dropped down dead that moment. Good thing they don't. First that face and now ... He got to his feet, looked up, and was standing nose to nose with Brother Bernard. They stared at each other across the open coffin.

Dead white, furious, Brother Bernard. I've never seen such anger.

'Thomas Wright, put him back!'

My father, shocked out of his mind, needing an answer.

'Brother, did you, was there really a face, did you see ...?'

'PUT HIM BACK! This is our Saint, what you are doing God knows but it is evil. Evil! Put Saint Thomas back. Now!'

'Brother Bernard, we can save him, we can exchange the ...'

But Brother Bernard had turned furiously away and was striding off to get help. We would have Father Prior on us any moment, maybe even the Archbishop.

Where were Ellie and Lipperty Jack? Nowhere. Must have run home. Simon and Joshua? Not a sign of them.

And then, then! my amazing father set to and worked like a whirlwind, like a dozen whirlwinds, to get all Saint Thomas's bones – most of his bones – out of the coffin. I decided I needn't hide any more, slid down the ladder and ran to help, shook Great Grandfather Harry out of the sack and held it open. Father gave me an astonished smile, rattled the Saint's bones into the sack, and there we were. He leant forward to put Great Grandfather into the coffin in some sort of order, ribs here, long bones there, skull at the top – yes, that shiny thing was a small chalice. I stowed the Saint's bones well down into the sack, picked the whole thing up and darted back out of the way.

As I stuffed them away I'd noticed a hole in the top of the Saint's skull, a bit missing. Yes, one of the murderers had slashed it off, that's right, I remembered the story. And Great Grandfather had died falling off scaffolding onto a stone floor, hit his head – two damaged skulls, when the king's men came they'd never realise they'd got the wrong one, if they even bothered to check. We were winning!

I was out of sight, not out of hearing. There came Brother Bernard again, I heard his voice.

'There he is, Father Prior, there he is! Thomas Wright, infamous, unforgivable, look at him! Evil!'

I risked a glance round a pillar. What Father Prior saw was an open coffin full of old dry bones, and a quiet defeated man sitting back on his heels, head bent, humbled. Waiting for punishment. My clever dad.

No one spoke for a bit. Then the Prior said:

'Thomas, what is this?' He took one of my father's hands and made him get up, then said again, 'What is this?' He'd known us all a long time, he knew Father wasn't evil.

Dad didn't answer straight away, but after a bit he just said, 'I wanted to save the Saint.'

'From the king's men?'

'Yes.'

'Thomas, dear man, you fool! I would never have thought that a man like you ... Have you no idea, don't you know ...?' There was a silence. It was as if all the dangerous things Father Prior must not say were roaring in his mind and trying to get said. No need to say them, we all knew. The king is a wolf, a lion, he is mad, he will kill us. His jaws drip blood. Keep quiet, keep quiet, wait.

Then the Prior patted my father on the shoulder and said, 'Put it all back. Close the coffin, put it back, make good the damage. Put it all back.' Then he turned and went away, calling Brother Bernard to go with him.

No one knew! No one had any idea we'd swapped the bones round. Father began to tidy up the coffin and close it, and I slipped quietly away with the sack. I don't think he saw me go.

I went to my best place, up the Bell Harry Tower and into the wheel loft. No one working there. My little shadow caught me up and helped with the sack, silent Lipperty. Where was Ellie? Gone home, I think.

I climbed into the treadmill, the great wheel, all locked up and still. There might be a corner, a hole, some cranny or other ... No, not safe enough. People work there. Away, a good long way away. We went – I'm not going to say where we went. A long way. Out of the wheel and then up, up, along ...

At one point we were going carefully along a high narrow passageway that's completely open on one side, you could topple down smash if you didn't take care, and suddenly there were people hurrying about far down below us ... we froze, stood like statues, but people never do look up, it was all right. To think I used to play along there for fun, and sometimes dropped cobnut shells on people's heads!

We got away from there and into the high timberwork. Yes, this was right. As far in as we could ... further ...

I climbed out and could hear Lippy pushing and rattling and ramming the sackful of bones into the furthest hiding place we could find. An amazing boy that, I wondered then and I still wonder what he thought we were doing.

Then out he came, all dusty, and we took hands and scrambled and ran all the way jumping and laughing till we got to the stairway, and so down and down and home and dinner. We were famished.

I thought of the face I'd seen, stern, terrible, and then how it vanished, just went, and I shivered.

Over second helpings of beef and dumplings my father looked at me and said, 'Oh by the way Harry, thanks for helping with the clearing up. Where exactly did you put that sack?'

'I don't know *exactly*,' I said. 'Somewhere up the Harry Tower. Safe. Lippy did it for me really, he knows.' We both looked at little Lipperty, silent, silent, silent, and smiled.

CHAPTER SEVEN
ARRESTED

Everything was all right. The Saint's bones were safe and no one knew. It was a good summer, cherries doing well and apples looking promising. Father's roses flowered and began to fall, Mother and Ellie picked them to dry the petals for their scent. Great Aunt Rose told them the proper way to treat them and they smiled and went on doing it the way they'd always done. Little Lucy could almost walk. Lipperty Jack still spoke never a word and we had no idea who he belonged to or how we could find out. Cat had kittens, three tabby and two ginger. Peter began to talk about moving to Germany or France where it was all right to read the Bible for yourself in your own language and he would be safer. He thought too that Mistress Cranmer would be able to help him get work, but in the end he stayed at home. We were very busy in the workshop. The Lord Archbishop had ordered a new lectern from us, one made to his own design to use when he was reading or writing. He hated sitting down to do anything, people said, was always on his feet.

Oh, Mistress Cranmer? She was the Archbishop's wife, but most of the time had to live abroad for safety's sake, because priests in England were not allowed to have a wife. Marry, and the king would have you hanged. In Germany it was all right.

I wasn't too sure about France being safe, and neither was Ellie. I remember she asked Peter about it once when we were sitting round the table at dinner. He laughed cheerfully and said:

'Oh yes, the French king doesn't mind reformers. That's the only way we can get the Holy Bible in our own language here, you know. King Francis lets them print pages in Paris, and then they're smuggled across to us here so that the blessed light of the Gospel can shine in England!' I noticed Father shaking his head, but he didn't say anything. Neither did I, but I knew the French were our enemies.

'Don't let our king catch them at it, that's all,' said Great Aunt Rose. 'Otherwise it's the fire for them.'

And she meant the people, not the books. King Harry might not like the pope but he didn't like Luther either.

There was a lot of quiet murmuring in the town about the monasteries, the small ones all over England that had been closed down already. Quiet, because talking was dangerous. Some people thought it was terrible, that beggars and wanderers, poor people, had nowhere to turn to nowadays, no one to give them shelter or food, but other people said it would do those fat monks no harm to get up off their backsides and do a real job of work.

And the big places would go too, we knew that. July was just about ending when the abbot of Saint Augustine's outside the city wall had to hand his abbey over to the king, and the king's men came and started tearing a lot of it down.

'They've even broken down the tomb of Saint Augustine himself,' said my mother, her eyes full of tears, 'our own first saint. Hundreds and hundreds of years he's lain there, ever since he brought Christ to the English, and now they shovel his blessed bones aside like so much trash.'

'All the same,' said Peter, 'it's a new clean world. There's a lot that had to go. What rubbishy tricks they get up to! Just imagine, that blood they have away there in Gloucestershire and pass it off as belonging to some saint or other, oh so holy, they get it from a duck. A duck, for goodness' sake!'

'Poor duck,' said my soft-hearted sister, and I wanted to know what happened to the duck next, did they cook it and have it for dinner? but I didn't ask.

It was late afternoon, the end of a fine day, and my uncle Joshua was with us. Mother was worried about him, what would he do when his monastery was closed down and they were all turned out onto the street?

'He'll come to us,' my father said. 'Of course he will, he's family. But what will you do, though? I don't see you as a carpenter.'

'He could teach music,' said Mother. 'At the school. The master knows you, doesn't he?'

'Oh yes,' said Joshua. 'And he likes music.'

'But two-faced!' put in Peter. 'Say anything about new ideas and reform, getting rid of relics, having the Bible in English, he'll say the opposite, but stand up for the old ideas and he'll contradict you on that! No one has any idea what Master Twyne really thinks.'

'Very clever!' said Great Aunt Rose. 'As long as he takes care not to fall off his tightrope.'

'No, sheer hypocrisy!' said Uncle Joshua. 'Dishonest, shameful! No earthly king can rule God's church! The Holy Father, the blessed pope, he's the head, the only head, of Christ's church, successor of Saint Peter, chosen by Christ himself. We are his servants and must proclaim the truth. If need be I will die for my faith.'

'But you don't actually want to, do you?' Ellie asked him, and he gave a sudden laugh and said no, of course not, and why didn't we have some music?

I'm not sure what my faith is, except the obvious

things like good and evil and heaven and hell and keeping your word and Father Benedict says you must do as you want to be done by, and I know God loves me otherwise he wouldn't have bothered to make me, but what I really want to do is to command a ship, a good neat fast little vessel, and take her to find gold in the new countries in the far off west. No one's going to bother about duck's blood there. And standing by your friends, that's important.

Mother was finishing off a shirt for Peter, and Ellie was sewing too, so they just sang, and the rest of us got out the recorders. Ellie had decided that little Lippy was growing and ought to have something to wear of his own, not just stuff I'd grown out of. Joshua is really good at music, he comes all alive then, and he keeps time and directs what we do.

Cat gave us a look and stalked off into the garden. The kittens didn't seem to take much notice.

'A song for the king!' said my uncle Josh, and he started us off into

Pastime and good company
I love and shall until I die!

A catchy tune, and we played and sang it round and round.

'King Harry wrote that himself, didn't he?' I said, and

thought that he must be all right really, to make a song like that.

'He did,' said my uncle. 'Other songs too. He's always been good at music. And in those days he was very different, a true son of Holy Church. More's the pity ... '

'For goodness sake, just sing!' cried my mother, and he laughed and started on a miserable old psalm tune, all wailing and sad, till Mother snatched up a wooden spoon and hit him with it. Not very hard.

We did old songs and new songs, church songs and every day songs, and little Lipperty sat by me cross-legged on the floor and tapped his hand on his knee in time with the music. Then, just as we were finishing off the *Summer* song with good loud shouts of 'Cuckoo! Cuckoo!' and we stopped – one voice was still singing. No words, just the tune, strong and sweet – it was Lipperty. Silent speechless Lippy. Tiny shy frightened Lippy, sitting there with a beaming smile and carolling away like a lark.

Ellie hugged him and even Great Aunt Rose laughed out loud.

And then footsteps outside. And knocking, very loud. We only had time to look at each other and wonder what on ... before the door crashed open and in came the king's men.

Five of them. One officer and four others. Father stood up and so did Peter. The rest of us stayed still.

'Thomas Wright, master of the cathedral workshop?' asked the officer, and my father nodded.

'Wanted for questioning,' said the man, and went on, 'Who are these others?' He looked down at a list in his hand and said, 'Brother Simon, we've got him. Is Joshua Stephens here?'

Dead white, my uncle got to his feet and said, 'Yes, I'm Joshua.'

My mother was angry. She folded her sewing over and laid it aside, then jumped up and asked how he dared come bursting in to take her husband and her brother away? What wrong had they ever done?

But the only answer she got was, 'Your brother, is he? You'd better keep quiet, girl, or we may find we need you too. Just don't get in our way.'

Peter moved across to stand beside Father.

'Where are you taking them?' he said. 'Why do you want them?'

'Young fool!' said the officer, and that was all.

'Leave it, Peter!' said my dad. 'Look after the young ones. Look after Clare.'

And that was it, over, done, they were gone.

It happened so quickly.

Ellie put out a hand to Peter and said, 'We should have stopped them!' and Peter gripped it but all he said was, 'How?'

I wasn't crying, not at all, but my eyes were wet and all

I could say was that I didn't understand. True enough, I didn't.

'None of us do,' said my mother, tears running down her face. 'None of us do. We must just be patient and hope and keep praying ...' She lifted baby Lucy out of her cot, held her close and began to rock her.

Lipperty crept out from under the table and clung to Mother's side.

I could see Ellie staring down at the sewing in her hands as if she had never set eyes on it before. Her needle had come unthreaded and she tried to rethread it, couldn't see past her tears and broke into a storm of sobs.

Great Aunt Rose looked round at us all. She shook her head and said, painfully, 'Whatever it is they accuse him of, he did it.'

Mother rounded on her in fury, called her a wicked old woman, how dared she say that?

'Wicked am I?' said my great aunt. 'Old too. But not stupid. I watched them. I watched Thomas. Didn't you see? When the men came for him, he *knew*. He wasn't surprised.'

CHAPTER EIGHT
KEEP QUIET

Our world had crumbled to bits. None of us knew what to do. Mother and Peter went to ask at the Castle if Father and Joshua were being held in the jail there, could they visit them, bring them food, were they all right? but no one knew anything. Or said they didn't. I went there once on my own and looked about, tried to find someone with a friendly face, but no, there wasn't one.

I came home and slid under the kitchen table to see if I couldn't sail a pretend ship to beat up the French or take a vessel north among the white bears – no, it was ridiculous. I was a child under a table and my father had been taken away and it wasn't safe to talk about it. No more ships.

I heard Peter's voice shouting for me and was glad to go and do some of the jobs he had lined up for me in the workshop.

We did keep that in business, just. Money was tight,

very tight, not everyone wanted to order furniture or building work from a family whose head was in prison. We sold Joe, the big horse, but kept Cobby. Peter and I sawed, planed, hammered, tightened up joints, smoothed rough surfaces, rounded off corners, did all we could. We worked up in the Bell Harry Tower, strengthening supports – at least Father Prior still trusted us, brave of him really. He put Johnny in charge of the cathedral works, our dad's job that was, but he kept Peter on, and I made myself useful.

Even in our own church, Saint Peter's, people kept their distance, edged away. Wherever we might stand to hear mass when we went in there, somehow there was always a space around us, no one very near.

'You can't expect it of them,' said Aunt Rose. 'They're terrified.'

Ellie didn't like it, though, when Father Benedict, kind Father Benedict! took her aside one day as we were coming out of Saint Peter's after church and explained to her that it would be better if she didn't take the part of the Virgin Mary in the Christmas play.

'But it's my turn!' she said, surprised. 'Anne did it last year and I remember you said ...'

'Yes,' he said, 'yes, but her mother thinks ...'

'Her mother,' said Great Aunt Rose, stamping up to him, 'should keep a more careful eye on that child. Virgin? I wonder!'

As the rest of the congregation, including Anne and her mother, brothers and sisters, were all just behind us in the porch, everyone heard this very clearly, and there were chokes of laughter and a startled silence. Then we stood aside and let Anne's family sweep by.

Aunt Rose sailed off after them and Father Benedict stood watching her go.

'What an Innkeeper's Wife she would make!' he said wistfully, and then, 'Dear Ellie, next year, soon, I promise you!'

I did a good deal in the garden, and we all helped harvest the peas and beans. Lipperty helped with that, and with the hens, but mostly I think he just concentrated on not being in anyone's way. He liked the little cats, and sometimes I noticed him sitting in the stable with Cobby, who was missing Joe, I knew he was. Cobby wouldn't expect him to talk.

Great Aunt Rose sat in her corner and helped out where she could – and she kept very quiet. If only we'd been happier, we'd have been glad of that.

Mother and Ellie were extra busy all the time in the house because Peggy Ann who worked for us had had to go home. Her mother wanted her back in Fordwich because it wasn't safe being anywhere around the Wrights. She didn't want to go, I'll give her that. What with all their usual work and baby Lucy to look after, and Peggy Ann's work on top of that, Mother and

Ellie and even Aunt Rose all had far too much to do – cooking, cleaning, washing, ironing, seeing to the hens, keeping our clothes mended or new ones made. New ones made, Ellie laughed at me when I said that, and told me it was more like turning the old clothes inside out and making them look as if they'd been new once upon a time. And the slop bucket, no one likes going round with that every morning, collecting all the slosh from the chamber pots and washing them out, but it has to be done. Luckily they decided I was too young, might spill them, and anyway I really did have all I could manage to do helping Peter.

The worst thing, Mother said, was going out to buy food at the market or in the shops. People she'd known all her life took care not to see her.

'It's as if I'd got leprosy!' she said once. 'Not fit to mix with them!'

'The king hates us,' said Aunt Rose. 'More deadly than leprosy. Anyone can catch it.'

'And we don't even know why,' said Peter, shaking his head.

I looked at Ellie and she looked at me. We knew why.

Well, I did. I knew where the Saint's bones were. I was the only person in the world who knew that. Except Lippy, if you can count him And Father, more or less.

What ought I do?

Easy, stay quiet.

Easy to say, easy to do?

Talk, and the king kills your dad. Shut up.

'What they all know very well indeed,' Mother said one day as she came in with a basket in each hand, 'is that a single word spoken against the king, a look, a hint, a breath, can whirl round and come back and murder you. Safer not to talk to us – not to see us.'

As she put the baskets down, Bell Harry rang out from the top of his tower to call the monks to prayer. It rings four times a day, my bell, and each time I heard it I stopped whatever I was doing, put my hands together and prayed aloud,

'Dear God, bring my father home safe. And Uncle Joshua.'

'Amen,' said my mother, and kissed me.

CHAPTER NINE
HOW CAN HE KNOW?

That same night we were all just sitting around, tired out, ready for bed, when someone tapped at the door. Not a knock, just a tap. We looked at each other. Ellie was nearest the door – she shrugged, and opened it.

Brother Bernard. He stood there, looked at Mother, then said, 'Mistress Wright. May I come in?'

'Of course.'

In he came, stood still and looked round at us. He was pale, anxious, seemed to want to say something but didn't know how – none of us had ever seen him like this, never. He wasn't that kind of man. We were all on our feet by now, and we waited.

Then at last:

'It must have been through me. When I saw Thomas there with the Saint's coffin open in front of him, I ... It was terrible, unholy, it should not be happening, but it was not treason. Not treason, not an offence against the king. Against the Saint, against the Church, perhaps against God, yes, but not against the king. I had no idea it would come to this. I rebuked Brother Joshua, I spoke to Brother Simon, but I never dreamt ... I want you to know that I never imagined ... The word got round, it reached the king's men, it must have come from me but I never intended ...'

He broke off and stopped talking. None of us were much the wiser.

'Brother Bernard,' said my mother after a bit, 'we have had no news of any kind.'

'Then you don't know ...'

'We don't know anything. Not where they are, or why, not anything. Weeks and weeks ... All summer, and now autumn ... Brother, for God's sake, tell us!'

I found I was holding Ellie's hand. We gripped tight.

Brother Bernard came further into the room and asked if he might sit down. Mother nodded. He sat down, laid his hands palms upwards on his knees, shut his eyes and, I thought, prayed. Then, opening his eyes again, he said:

'Children, Thomas and Brother Joshua are accused of treason. High treason. Crime against the king. Of attempting to save the bones of Bishop Becket – the Saint, Bishop Becket, that's what we have to call him now – from the king's men. From destruction. They are being held prisoner in London. In Southwark, I believe.' He blinked his eyes shut again, pulled himself together and went on, 'It has not been easy for them. They have suffered.'

'Put to the torture, you mean?' asked Peter in a low voice. Bernard nodded.

'Yes, I believe so,' he said. 'They have both refused to name any other conspirators.'

Conspirators? But there was no conspiracy, just my father and me, with Simon and Joshua on guard. Is that a conspiracy?

I went on keeping quiet.

Brother Bernard was talking again.

'Brother Simon has come home. He was arrested and questioned but has been released. He's here in the priory now, in the, in the infirmary. The judge decided he was not involved in the actual attempt at theft, only accidentally caught up in it. Simon is free.'

'My husband?' asked Mother. 'And my brother? What have they decided?'

'Nothing as yet. All they know is that Thomas opened the Saint's coffin, and then when he was told to, shut it again. He never touched the Saint's bones, he was only intending to remove them. So they say.'

They knew that, did they? I knew different! And kept quiet.

'And that Brother Joshua was with him at the time,'

Brother Bernard went on, 'apparently keeping watch. Thomas admits that he wanted to take the Saint's bones away, but that's all he does say. He refuses to say why, or to name anyone else involved. He insists that there was no one else, that it was all his own idea. Father Prior was called, and his own parish priest from Saint Peter's, Father Benedict, they both spoke up for him. So did I. I was summoned as a witness and I told them the truth, that he had never had the name of a fanatic, just a straightforward honest man.'

'So he is,' said Great Aunt Rose, 'so he is. And stupid,' she muttered angrily under her breath, 'stupid.'

'What will happen now?' asked Peter.

'We wait. They are being held in prison, both of them, until the judges name another day for going on with the trial. The courts are full, these days. There are so many people under suspicion. Lord Cromwell is determined to root out all taint of treason.'

'Lord Cromwell?' asked my mother.

'Master Secretary Cromwell, the king's great minister. Another Thomas!' said Brother Bernard with an attempt at a smile.

'I remember seeing the king when he was young,' said my mother, shaking her head unhappily. 'Such a handsome smiling lad, so friendly, so kind … How can he know everything that goes on, the things people do in his name?'

CHAPTER TEN
FIND THE KING

'I wonder if this Master Cromwell likes managing things his own way,' my mother went on. 'Perhaps he doesn't always tell King Harry everything. Surely the king would be merciful if he knew ... ?'

'Don't pin your hopes to that, dear Mistress Wright,' said Brother Bernard. 'Master Thomas doesn't manage the king. No one does.'

'The Cardinal thought he did, in the olden days, didn't he?' said Great Aunt Rose. 'Ruled the whole country and got fat and rich while the king rode horses and chased women. And look where that got him. This Master Secretary has the same idea now, but we'll see, we'll see.'

'Never mind that,' said my mother. 'Brother Bernard, if I can get to London, shall I be able to see them? Will they let me into the prison ?'

'I think not,' he said, looking rather alarmed. 'I do not advise it, I really do not.' He caught Peter's eye, murmured to him, 'Don't let her, don't let her,' and all in the same breath said that he really must be going now and would let her have any news the moment he received it.

He turned towards the door just as Peter burst out in an exclamation against Joshua. My poor Uncle Josh, in prison, perhaps being tortured, perhaps going to die and Peter calls him names!

'Stupid Joshua, stupid!' he was muttering. 'Pious young fool, clinging to that old nonsense, when the true light of the Gospel is shining out of Germany! How can he be so blind?'

Brother Bernard swung round in the doorway and listened to him.

'Germany?' he said sharply. 'You mean Martin Luther, that piece of filth, that stinking fool? Enemy of the pope, of the king, of God Almighty! Peter Wright, if your family didn't need you here now to earn some bread, I'd inform against you myself. If you can't see sense, at least keep quiet, if only for the children's sake!'

'I know, I know!' said my fool of a grown up brother. 'But just for some nonsensical relics, and he drags our father ...'

I couldn't keep quiet then, it was either shout or

burst into tears so I shouted. Told him that was my mother's own brother he was calling names, couldn't he think about her, shut his big mouth, and while Father was – I ran out of words there, and stopped. Peter gawped at me, and shut up. Brother Bernard said quietly, 'Good advice, good advice. God keep you all', and went.

Peter began to try to explain himself to Mother, but Great Aunt Rose told him sharply to save his breath to cool his porridge, and he did stop then.

We went to bed.

I lay awake and went over things in my mind. Bones. The sack. Great Grandfather. Lying on the canopy high up above the Black Prince and watching. That sudden face. Yes, it had all happened. We had saved the Saint's bones. I knew, so did Father, so in an odd way did Lipperty, but no one else, not even Ellie.

If the king knew ...

He must not.

Never, never, never.

But I needed to find the king.

The important thing as I saw it, the only important thing, was that my father was a good man, and King Harry didn't know this. What anybody had done or not done, never mind, my father is good, and how could the king know that? Of course he couldn't. If he did know, if I went and told him, he would have my father set free. Only bad men should be in prison. Plain common sense.

How young I was, how ignorant and silly!

I had no idea, thank God.

CHAPTER ELEVEN
DESTRUCTION

I woke up knowing what I had to do, but not how to do it. Go and find the king.

Yes. Where?

And meanwhile I had Peter shouting for me to come and get on with stuff in the workshop.

'Check those timbers for knots,' he said. 'Sort out which are worth rubbing down and keeping, and which ones aren't.'

Six were not too bad, four had loose knots or even knotholes in them, and I stacked them into two lots. It took me all morning to get the six good ones smooth. Peter was working on the panelling that was meant for the Prior's house.

'Though if Father Prior has to go, he's not going to want new panelling, is he?' I heard him say to himself. 'But his house won't disappear, someone will need it.

Better get it done. Hope someone pays us.'

I'd done all I could on the six lengths of timber, sharpened a couple of chisels, swept up and that was it. Peter looked up from the pattern he was gouging along a section of the panelling and gave me a bleak smile.

'The big plane needs resetting,' he said, 'but I'll see to that. You be off, give yourself a holiday. There are no more orders coming in. Just these panels to finish and install, and then that's it. No more to do.'

No orders, no work, no money. How shall we live? I had to find the king!

It was dinner time. Mostly bread, and an onion and a bit of cheese. I knew better than to grumble. If I didn't get to explain things to King Harry, there wouldn't even be that.

Then it came to me – ask the Saint. He's in his cathedral. He knows all about it, go and ask him what to do.

I put my head round the kitchen door, told Mother I was just going out for something, and was off. No sign of Lippy, probably talking to Cobby, fine.

I went in by the usual side door, crossed myself and shut my eyes. No need to go all the way up the tower to find the hidden sack, I was in the Saint's own cathedral, he would hear me. He knew what we'd done for him.

'Blessed Saint Thomas,' I said under my breath, 'pray for us! Holy Saint Thomas, pray for us and help us and look out for my Great Grandfather! Help my father! Tell me where to find the king!'

I walked on and had a look at my favourite window, the one where some boys have been throwing stones at frogs and one of them gets drowned, Robert he was called, but the Saint brings him back to life. Huge frogs they are, not surprised they threw stones at them. I caught sight of the Three Kings window too, all three of them peacefully asleep with their golden crowns glittering. Uncomfortable, I used to think.

'Saint Thomas,' I said again into the silence, 'help my father! And tell me what to ...'

A crashing noise, a sudden crashing and banging over by the Saint's tomb. Loud voices too. I moved carefully round a pillar and looked.

Men working at the Saint's tomb. Men using claw hammers, wrenches, crowbars, all sorts, and they were breaking the shrine to bits, taking all the gold and jewels and stuff off it and packing it into boxes. They were busy and cheerful, whistling. One of them was hard at work making a list of every item.

And there were armed men there too, big solid men with swords and axes, keeping watch. I didn't like the look of them at all. Nor of their dogs, big fierce creatures with spiky collars, four of them and two of the guards holding them on leashes.

'God, look at this one!' said one of the men, lifting

some treasure off the shrine. 'Worth a king's ransom, I wouldn't wonder.'

'Get on with it,' said the one making the list. 'And be careful. That's a famous one, the Regale. Damage that, and you'd be better jumping off the top of the tower.'

I knew that jewel, of course I did. A king of France had given it long long ago, when his son was ill and he wanted Saint Thomas to heal him.

I went away. Silly thoughts skittered about in my head, like, What will they do with the Icelandic chieftain's walrus tusk? but mainly I just felt stupid. And I still had no idea how to find King Harry, how I could even start to look for him.

Down the Pilgrims' Steps and out through the south door – and I stopped in amazement. Half Canterbury was standing there, a whole silent crowd, a line of people three or four deep, stretching round the Cathedral as far as I could see. There were armed men posted to stop them getting in, but I don't think any of them wanted to, they had just come to watch. To see the Saint go. To say goodbye.

Someone waved and it was Ellie. She and Mother and Lippy were standing there, even Great Aunt Rose was there, and I ran across to join them.

We stood and stood. Someone came out from one of the houses and brought a stool for Aunt Rose.

Barrow load after barrow load was carried out from

the cathedral, chests and boxes were loaded up onto carts and driven away. More than twenty carts, someone said. Never ending.

At long last a man came out carrying just one sack, and the guards and dog-handlers came close behind him.

People in the crowd muttered, broke the silence.

'It's the bones! It's the Saint himself! There he goes!' I heard all sorts. 'Good riddance! God save the king!' from some, 'God forgive us, God help us!' from others.

The man tossed the sack up onto the last cart, climbed up after it and turned to look at the crowd. He smiled, raised a fist and shook it, shouted out:

'So perish all the king's enemies!' and then the cart and the whole troop moved off.

'It's the end of the world,' said Great Aunt Rose, tears trickling down her old face.

I found I was crying too, and inside my head I was saying things like, 'Grandfather, sorry, thank you! Saint Thomas, take care of him!' but I kept my mouth tight shut.

I must not tell them. Must not.

Ellie choked back her sobs and said half aloud, 'If only we had managed it, if only!'

I hugged her and didn't say anything except, 'Come on, let's go home.'

CHAPTER TWELVE
TRY MEISTER OMERS

This one huge fact sat in my mind like a toad and laughed at me. I know where the Saint's bones were. Ha ha, all you idiots, I can tell you a thing or two.

Tell no one, no one, don't be a fool.

Bit by bit I wrapped that toad up in a bundle of common sense and forced it to the back of my mind, put it in a cupboard there and turned the key in the door.

Done, safe.

But I still needed to find the king and explain to him that his officials had made a mistake, they had put a good man in jail. Uncle Joshua too, he was good, good through and through, he just didn't think the same way the king did. The king would order Secretary Cromwell to have both of them set free as soon as he understood that, I was sure he would. My God, how young I was!

My mother was in the kitchen, ironing. Well, why not ask her?

'Mother, I need to go and see the king. How can I find out where he is?' She put her iron down by the fire and stared at me.

'My darling silly boy, are you ill?'

'No, but I need to tell him about Father. Like you said, he probably doesn't know, that Secretary man won't tell him what goes on, but I can, I will, only I don't know where to start looking for him. Who do you think I can ask, who will know?'

'Father Prior,' she said doubtfully, folding up a shirt. 'And the Archbishop. All sorts of grand people, people we can't talk to. Can't get near. The king lives in London.'

'And in Greenwich,' chipped in Great Aunt Rose from her corner by the fire. 'And in Hampton Court. All over the place. Kings travel, that's what they do. They go to one place and eat up all the food until the cupboards are empty and then they move on.'

I thought that would make them ill, but Mother explained that kings never went anywhere alone, they always had dozens and dozens of lords and ladies and servants and soldiers, and all of them did a lot of eating.

'Drinking too,' said Aunt Rose. 'And not just dozens, more like hundreds, and all of them on the make and wanting money before they'll let you anywhere near the king.'

Wanting money, that's a problem, I thought. But if I got to the right place ...

I was small, I could dodge past people. Just needed to know where.

I went out of the kitchen, still wondering, and heard my sister running after me.

'I'm coming with you,' she said.

'Not if you're going to boss me about.'

'Of course not! Do I ever?' I laughed at that, but didn't answer back, things were too serious.

'You can come if you like,' I said, 'but why? What good will you be?'

'Two's better than one. I can – I can stand on my head and make people look at me while you sneak through to the king. Or dance. Or sing songs.'

'Or scream. So you can. All right, we'll go together, the two of us. Three of us,' I added, looking down at Lipperty who was clutching my hand. 'But where?'

'We could try the palace he's having built at St Augustine's,' said Ellie. 'He won't be there yet, it's all full of workmen pulling the old stuff down and that, but people might know when he's due to come there.'

'We've no time to waste!'

People die under torture. I knew that. So did Ellie. Neither of us said it aloud.

We began to run softly towards the Cathedral. If you go right past it, you come to a small gate in the city wall, and St Augustine's is just on the other side. Lippy held onto my hand and hopped along. He was much more cheerful nowadays but still didn't speak. He very nearly did once, playing with the kittens – I saw him stroking one of the ginger ones and making the shape of a word with his lips, and I dropped down beside him and told him what it was called. 'Kitten,' I said carefully, 'kitten, that's a kitten, that is. Kitten.' Ellie heard me and laughed, told me not to try too hard,

'It'll come when he's ready. Don't fuss him!'

'Oh no,' said Ellie suddenly. 'Not St Augustine's, Meister Omers.' We'd passed the Cathedral by now and there was the house we call Meister Omers over on our left, and yes, that made sense, grand people often went and stayed there.

'Right,' I said, and we veered off towards it.

'My friend Sarah works in the kitchens there,' said Ellie. 'We'll ask her.'

We went round to the back door. It was shut.

Ellie knocked. No one came. She knocked again and I knocked too, even Lipperty did a bit of banging.

'Plenty of people in there,' I said. 'Just listen to the racket.' Pots and pans, shouts, laughter.

'They can't hear us,' said Ellie. 'Let's open the door.'

The latch was stiff and I struggled with it. Suddenly it sprang open under my hands and there was a tall greasy boy looking down at us. He broke into a laugh, said, 'No beggars, no clowns, no gypsies!' and slammed the door shut.

'You dare!' said Ellie, and she fought it open again. In we marched, the three of us, and Ellie went on, 'We just want to see Sarah. Is she here?' By now all the talking and laughing had stopped and a crowd of cooks and scullions and what not were looking at us.

'No,' said a fat woman, 'Sarah's not here. Why d'you want her?' No business of hers, that!

'We wanted to ask her if the king was coming,' said Ellie. 'Do you know, can you tell us?'

'The king!' said the fat woman. 'The king, oh my dear soul and you come to the back door, noble people like you and wanting to see the king, oh deary me what a mistake!'

How they all laughed!

'Laugh like that, you'll wet yourselves!' I shouted, at the same time as Ellie was saying, 'We need to tell him ...'

'Tell him the sky is falling down!' screamed the fat woman, and kept on laughing.

'I can help you!' shouted the greasy boy, and he seized a round baking tin and set it on his head, grabbed a poker in one hand and an apple in the other, then hitched himself up onto a table. He sat there sticking his legs out and roaring at how funny he thought he was.

'I am the king!' he shouted. 'Down on your mucky

little knees, grubbikins, downsywownsy and kiss the floor!' He sprang off the table, turned round and stuck out his bottom at us. 'You can kiss my backside too, kissy kissy, come on quick!'

I bit him. I'm still good and pleased when I think of it. I lunged forward and sank my teeth into the back of his thigh, just where it's soft, and he screamed and leapt up and grabbed me by the throat. Not so funny. Ellie wrapped herself round his legs and brought him crashing down to the ground and Lippy was jumping up and down yelling – yelling, our silent Lippy? I didn't think about that then.

Anyway, it all stopped. A man at the back of the room said just the one word, 'Out!' and everything went quiet.

'Out!' he said again. 'I know who you are, you're Thomas Wright's brats, Thomas the traitor. We don't want your sort here. Scully, stop playing the fool, open the door and kick them out, then get on with your work.'

We trailed away, fuming.

'Home?' said Ellie.

'Not yet,' I said. 'We can still try St Augustine's.'

But we couldn't.

When we got to the little gate, Queen Bertha's gate, it was guarded. No one could go through either way without a written pass.

We stood and looked at it.

'Must be dinner time,' I said feebly. 'May as well go

home.' As we stood looking, a tall figure came in through the gate, striding fast, and then after him another man. The second one was Father Prior, and the one in front – I didn't see who it was at first, but Ellie did.

'Look,' she said, 'look! It's Master Cranmer, it's the Lord Archbishop.'

'He'll know if anyone does,' I said. I did hesitate, I know I did, but then I remembered Father in prison and being torn apart on the rack, and I stepped in front of them, so that they both had to stop.

'Sir,' I said, 'Sir, my lord, it's my father, can you tell us where we can find ...'

This was not the clearest of questions, I know that! I muttered and mumbled and Ellie never told me so afterwards, for once my kind sister.

I think the Archbishop thought we were beggar children. Being rolled about on a kitchen floor does make you look a bit rough. Father Prior knew us, of course, but he and Lord Cranmer were in a hurry, busy, I don't know – they didn't listen.

The Archbishop tossed us a coin, raised a hand to bless us and walked on. Father Prior just nodded at us and said, 'Go home, children, go home and help your mother.'

So we went.

CHAPTER THIRTEEN
MARMALADE

We were just finishing what dinner there was when Brother Simon arrived. Ellie ran to hug him, but backed off when she saw the crutches – he was hobbling along, and trying to pretend none of it really mattered.

'No, no, no, nonsense,' was all he would say. 'I've come to talk about Thomas and Brother Joshua, not about me. Here, Harry, take this basket will you? What with that and the crutches ...'

I put the big covered basket down on the table. Simon didn't say much. He was sure Thomas and Joshua would be home soon, and neither of them were really badly hurt. They sent their dearest love to Clare and Peter and Ellie and Harry and baby Lucy – oh, and Aunt Rose – and everyone, and told them not to worry too much. No, of course the food there was horrible. And not enough of it. And everything stank to high heaven.

Beds? Simon almost laughed at a question from Clare:

'Beds, what beds? Dirty straw. But be glad they're alive! And think of St Peter,' he went on, moving restlessly from one foot to the other, 'and the way God just knocked the prison walls down for him and they could all walk out. You pray to your name-saint, young Peter, and ask him to help!'

I saw Peter tighten his lips and knew that he was keeping back his usual reply to that sort of remark: 'I don't pray to saints, I pray to God!'

Brother Simon must have noticed this too, because he rattled straight on to something different:

'But you're not all here, where's Peggy Ann? Is she all right?'

Mother explained that she had had to go home to Fordwich, and Great Aunt Rose joined in with one of her moans.

'No loyalty at all, young people, these days. No loss anyway, silly giggling goose, better off without her.' Mother looked daggers at old mumble grumble, but didn't speak. One of these days she'll throw something at her. Or I will.

'She didn't want to go,' said Ellie.

'Of course she didn't,' said my mother briskly, then changed the subject: 'Brother Simon, what have you brought us in that basket?'

'Ah, yes, that.' He took the cover off the basket – I'd

looked in straight away, there was nothing there but fruit, quinces, sour – and said, 'This is for you. No, wait a minute, I must tell you why. It's autumn now, quinces ripening, and listen, if ever you can get near the king, remember this: *he likes marmalade.*'

Mother gazed at him in astonishment, and could only say, 'Likes marmalade. And so?' Brother Simon smiled at her.

'It's just a chance. But you're a wonderful cook and there's an excellent crop in the abbey gardens this year, it was a good hot summer, and I've talked to Father Prior about it. He sends you these with his blessing. And sugar. From the priory store cupboards.'

'*Sugar*? Who can ever afford to buy sugar? Dear Simon, am I on my head or my heels?'

Great Aunt Rose got to her feet – not a thing she very often did – and stalked across to the basket. She prodded the fruit, sniffed it, and said grumpily, 'I've seen worse. If you don't know how to use it, girl, I do. I'll show you. I remember teaching Priscilla and she did very well with it, though we didn't use sugar, used honey.'

'I've never made it,' said my mother, 'never tried. But Brother Simon's right, I am a good cook, and we'll do it!'

'Good chewy sweets, mind!' said Aunt Rose. 'None of your sloppy mush.'

Peter said he had to get the Priory panels delivered and installed, and no, he didn't need me to help him.

'Stay here and get sticky,' he said, and went off muttering to himself.

'Two kinds,' said Great Aunt Rose. 'You can make two kinds, red or white.'

'How?' said my mother. 'Do you put colouring in?'

'Certainly not, no. What matters is how you do it. Simmer the quinces till they're tender, peel them as soon as they're cool enough to handle, then boil them up with the sugar, that's all. Boil it slowly for the red and fast for the white. Pour it out, let it cool, and cut it up into lozenges.'

'Make both,' said Ellie, 'make both and then they'll look pretty arranged side by side. Or in a pattern.'

It looked like a long job, this, and Lippy and I couldn't really help. I did offer to break up the chunks of sugar, but the women didn't want us around.

We went into the workshop – it felt all wrong, empty, no one there, no work, nothing. I picked up a chisel and mallet and began splitting short lengths of oak into thin rods to make pegs, and Lippy got busy in a corner using some odds and ends to build himself a small castle. It was not a bad castle, with ramparts and battlements and guns sticking out of loopholes, and for a while I flicked pellets of wood at it, knocking down some of the defences, and Lippy built them up again quick as a flash. But what was the point?

We went and mucked out Cobby's stable, although it didn't really need it. Cobby was pleased to see us.

They finished the white marmalade that afternoon but the red had to be boiled twice, a hot messy business, keeping it cooking and not letting it stick and burn. Mother poured it carefully out, a beautiful deep red, onto a marble slab where it could cool down and then be cut into squares. It smelt wonderful, it really did. I wondered how soon we could cut it up, but Mother said not until tomorrow, and she was going to lock the storeroom door. As if I would!

That was another day without knowing where I could even start looking for King Harry.

CHAPTER FOURTEEN
HE'S COMING

When Peter came back from the Prior's house, panels all safely installed and looking good, he was more cheerful. He'd seen Father Prior himself, he said, and felt sorry for him, he was so obviously a tired old man on his way out.

'He likes the panelling,' Peter said, 'of course he does, but it made him sad – said he was sure his successor would be glad of it and would see that it was properly cared for. And he knew all about Father and Uncle Joshua, told me to try not to worry and he was doing what he could.'

'And we've been doing what we can too,' said Ellie. 'There's two trays of quince sweeties cooling in the larder, and tomorrow we'll cut them up.'

'If they've set properly,' said Great Aunt Rose. 'Help me up the stairs, some of you, I should have been in my bed hours ago.'

'I'll make a box to put them in,' said Peter. 'Something small and neat. Better than doing nothing.'

Next morning we were all busy. Peter had put the glue-pot by the fire to soften and was in the workshop rubbing down a fine piece of pale oak. Ellie was sitting at one end of the kitchen table carefully drawing a picture of a rose, one which Peter would use to make a carving on the lid of the box. Mother was cutting the set slabs of quince paste into long strips, and then cutting them across to make lozenges, and Lipperty and I were taking turns with the pestle and mortar and were pounding little scraps of sugar down into a fine powder. This would be scattered on top of the sweets to stop them sticking to each other. I kept an eye on Lippy, but he didn't lick his fingers once, not once. Nor did I, of course but I knew how important this could be, and Lippy couldn't have any idea. I wondered again what could possibly be going on inside his head, and who it was that had lost him, and whether they minded or not.

'We'll soon have it ready to give the king,' said Ellie, shading in a delicate line on her picture. 'Mother, however do we manage to find out where the king is, and how do we get there?'

That's what I wanted to know too, indeed I did.

'All I can think of,' said Mother, edging her knife under the cut slabs to loosen them, 'is that we ask

Brother Bernard to ask Father Prior, and see if he can tell us.'

'And soon!' said I, banging gently down onto the crushed bits of sugar. 'Soon! It's been so long, and it must be so dreadful ...' So dreadful for Father and Uncle Josh, I was going to say, but I caught sight of Mother's face and stopped. 'I'll go and look for Brother Bernard the minute I've finished this,' I said instead. But she didn't want me to.

'No no, I'll talk to him,' she said. 'People don't always listen to a child.'

'They don't always listen to a woman either,' Ellie joined in. 'Hadn't it better be Peter? He's grown up, and he's a man.'

Mumble grumble aunt couldn't let that one pass, she gave a snort of a laugh and said, 'Peter! I should think not, we're in enough trouble already.' Peter caught his own name through the open door and appeared in the workshop doorway with the big plane in his hand. 'There's Thomas and Joshua in jail for siding with the pope and Saint Thomas,' Aunt Rose went on, 'and here's Peter risking being burnt to death by reading the Holy Bible in English, and as if that wasn't enough he keeps singing the praises of that fool heretic Luther. We're between a rock and a hard place, we are. Peter needs to keep quiet.'

Peter glared at Aunt Rose and said, not loud, 'The

piece I read in the Bible today told me I wasn't loving God properly if I didn't love my brother.'

'Quite right!' said the old lady. 'You don't need to be a heretic bound for the flames of hell to know that.'

'Great aunts,' said Peter, 'were not mentioned!'

Even Aunt Rose laughed then and Peter smiled and said he would pray for extra grace, he could see it was needed.

There was a sudden knock at the door, but it was only Brother Simon.

'Just the person we need,' said my mother, and asked him to find us a piece of good clean parchment. 'A big one we can cut into two,' she said. 'Look, it's to line the box Peter's making to put sweets in for the king. Here, have a trimming and tell me if it isn't good!'

She handed him a tiny scrap and he sniffed it, licked it, then put it in his mouth and exclaimed, 'Quince! Delicious!'

'What about us?' I said. 'Look how hard we've been working, and not a lick, not a sniff, nothing!' Mother laughed and handed out very small bits all round, baby Lucy included. It really was good, and even Aunt Rose had a job keeping the smile off her face.

Then came a surprise.

'How did you know?' asked Brother Simon.

'Know what?' said Mother.

'That the king's coming.'

'The king? Coming here? *Here*?'

'Yes, of course. Isn't that why you're making the marmalade? To give to him?'

'Well yes, but we didn't know ...'

'They're running round like headless chickens in Meister Omers, I can tell you. He means to stay there for several days, him and all his court, dozens and dozens of them, hundreds, and it's because there's some Frenchman or other coming over from France and it's important to make a fuss of him.'

'Important to welcome him in a proper manner,' said a new voice, and Brother Bernard came in through the open front door. 'May I come in, Mistress Wright?' She nodded, of course he could. Brother Simon stood up straight and looked respectful. 'The king and his court will stay in Meister Omers and receive the French guest and his followers there. A duke, I believe. And while King Henry is here he'll want to inspect the building operations going on at what used to be St Augustine's abbey. I am sure you know he's having it converted into a royal palace for himself and his guests, ambassadors, visiting nobles and such. So there will be several opportunities of seeing his grace, perhaps even of speaking to him.'

'But the French are our enemies!' I exclaimed. I didn't mean to say it aloud, it was just something I was thinking, something I knew, and it slipped out. Brother

Bernard looked at me as if I was a worm in his salad, and said, 'I came to tell you, Mistress Wright, about the king's visit, and that you should have a good chance of getting near him to offer a petition, to ask for mercy for your husband and your brother. But I do advise you to keep young Harry out of the way. He has no idea how to keep his mouth shut.'

That's what he thought.

CHAPTER FIFTEEN
PETITION

Next morning:

'The French,' said my mother, 'are *not* our enemies. Not. We are not at war with anyone, not even the Scots. We Have No Enemies.'

This was rubbish. We always hate the French. I could say we were even afraid of them, but it doesn't do to think of being afraid, no, we just hate them. They fight us, we fight them. They attack our ships and burn our towns. Murderers. All I could think of to say was, 'They always used to be.'

Great Aunt chipped in:

'And they will be again, don't you worry about that. All your mother means is that just at the moment there is no actual war and if King Harry wants to be polite to a visiting Frog, well then, that's his business.'

'They burned Rye,' I said.

'A hundred years ago!' said Peter. 'Look, I've finished carving Ellie's rose, what do you think?'

'And Winchelsea,' I went on, not giving in. 'They kill us.'

'And we kill them!' said my brother. 'But not all the time. Will you all of you look at our lid!'

Ellie was looking already, and you could see she was fizzing with pride. It really was a beautiful little thing, that lid, with its clever curving rose flowering on it.

'A Tudor rose, special for King Harry Tudor,' said Peter, and Ellie laughed and said she'd never thought about that, just liked roses.

'Where's the base?' said Peter, looking around. 'Oh, there it is.' He fitted the top and the bottom together and shook them gently. 'There, you see, fits like a dream, no rattle, no slopping about, perfect. Is the king here yet?'

'Not till tomorrow,' said my mother. 'We've time to write the petition as well. Peter, you'll do that, won't you? and the sweets are dry, we can start putting them in the box. Where's the parchment? Oh, here.' She laid one of the cut pieces carefully into the box and smoothed it into the corners. 'Now, Ellie, you and Harry put the sweets in. Make a pattern, stripy or zigzag, and be very, very gentle. And don't lick your fingers!'

'Of course not,' we murmured, and took turns placing the red and the creamy-coloured sweets as beautifully as we could. I did the red ones and Ellie did the white. When the bottom layer was done, red stripes side by side with white stripes, Mother laid the other piece of parchment over that and we did the top layer. Zigzags, that one.

'Put the lid on,' said Peter, handing it to Ellie, and she put it in place, hardly daring to breathe. Then she clapped her hands and burst out laughing, and we all laughed, except that I think one or two of us cried a bit.

Peter made the sign of the cross over our box of sweets and said, 'God send King Harry be kind and merciful!'

'Amen, amen!' we all said, and hugged each other.

'And fond of sweets and in a good temper!' my brother went on. 'I'll do that petition now, shall I? What exactly do I need to say?'

'You have to call him Majesty,' said Mother. 'Brother Bernard told me that, kings aren't Your Grace any more, they're Your Majesty. You could start off, *Most gracious Majesty, we your humble servants Peter and Harry Wright, sons of Thomas Wright of Canterbury, Master Carpenter, implore ...*'

I quite liked having my name in there, but Ellie interrupted, she thought Mother's name and hers and Lucy's ought to come in too, and Great Aunt Rose had something important to say:

'Listen, you stupid children, listen. The king doesn't

like men who have sons. Talk about Peter and Harry, and he will hate Thomas. He'll be jealous. Yes, I tell you, he will. He was married twenty, no, nineteen years ago to Queen Catherine, and poor lady, her babies died. Died and died and died. Just one of them lived, the Lady Mary. And he has had two more wives since then, and what has he got? One more daughter and a rickety little son, Prince Edward, and I shall be very surprised if that one makes old bones. No, whatever you say to King Harry, don't mention sons.'

'All this talk, talk, talk!' burst out my mother. 'There's my Thomas in prison, my brother too, no proper food, ill I daresay, perhaps even pulled to pieces on the rack – oh, do we have to go on talking? Can't we get on with it?'

'Yes, right,' said Peter. 'No sons. I'll do a rough draft now, and show you.'

He cleared a space on the table and got down to it.

'Green and white,' said Great Aunt Rose. 'Green and white, Tudor colours,' she added, seeing our puzzled looks. 'I've got a green ribbon if you've got a white one. We can tie the petition with them.'

There was nothing I could do, so I went to see if the hens had laid any eggs since the last time they'd been checked. Time to shut them up anyway. Lippy came with me. We made sure the hens were all in their shed and shut the door. Seven eggs. Came back in, put the bowl down and went and sat under the table. Lippy close by me. People's legs and feet all around. Big feet, planted firmly, a bit splay, Peter. Mother, pretty shoes, trodden over. Ellie, bare brown feet. I rocked gently to and fro where I sat and listened to Peter reading out what he'd written:

'Most gracious Majesty, your humble servant Clare, wife of Thomas Wright, Master Carpenter, in the parish of Saint Peter in the city of Canterbury, earnestly begs you to look kindly upon her husband the said Thomas now held in your royal prison in Southwark and upon Joshua Stephens her brother held with him, and to have mercy on them both and forgive them their offences and have them set free so that they may come home to those who love them and who will all their lives long pray to God for the health and happiness of your most noble Majesty, as well in body as in soul. This is the prayer of your humble subject and servant —

And then there's a space for you to put your mark, and after that it says

— Clare Wright, her mark.'

I'd listened carefully, and now I called out, 'But you haven't said that they didn't do anything wrong.'

'I know,' said Peter. 'I thought I'd better not touch that.'

CHAPTER SIXTEEN
FACE TO FACE

He was fat.

Huge.

Fatter than fat.

I'd never imagined. And tall, very very tall, enormous. No crown, just a big feathery velvety hat, but he didn't need a crown, he was solid king, anyone could see.

Red hair, red, I hadn't realised that.

Huge.

Rich and glittering with gold and jewels.

Everyone glittered, not us of course, I mean the lords and ladies standing around the king, and the other group moving towards him –

King Harry and his courtiers were standing outside Meister Omers, smiling and talking and looking welcoming, and the French duke and all his grand people were walking towards the king and looking more pleased and polite than anyone can imagine. The duke stopped still, swept off his splendid hat and made a low bow. All the men with him swept their hats off too and bowed, and the women curtsied. Our people bowed too, and curtsied, but not nearly as low as the French had done, and I noticed that King Harry kept his hat on.

'They don't have to like each other, do they?' I murmured to Ellie, just beside me, and she shook her head and said, 'Just play-acting. Don't they do it well?'

All the cathedral bells were ringing, I could hear my Bell Harry among them. They sang and clanged and jangled, making a joyful noise to welcome King Harry, lord of all England. Cross him and you die.

All Canterbury was there to see him.

It was all very well standing here gawping, but how do we get near him? Mother had the petition neatly rolled up and tied with green and white ribbons, Ellie had the carved box full of sweetmeats, wrapped in a cloth to keep it safe from sweaty hands, but none of us could see how to get any further. King Harry's large strong soldiers were standing on guard, not letting anyone come forward. They had long heavy pikes in their hands and were holding them lowered, held crisscross so as to make a sort of fence.

Mother did try. I heard her say, 'Sir, sir,' to the nearest pikeman, 'I have a petition to make to the king, I must see him, I must!'

All she got was, 'Petitions go to the Secretary. Wait till the meeting's over and they've all gone indoors, then hand it in.'

'No, that's no good, I must see the king himself. Please let me by!' But he didn't even look at her, let alone answer, just stood there like a rock, his pike laid across in front of her.

No, this was too much. Ellie and I looked at each other, nodded, ducked under the pike and ran forward. Lipperty scuttled after us.

A voice or two were shouting, 'Hey you!' but we three were kneeling in front of King Harry. None of us spoke. Ellie shook the wrappings off the box and held it up towards him. He looked down, puzzled.

I could see him thinking, truly I could, thinking, Is this a specially planned treat, three dear little angels kneeling before me, or are they stupid brats who need a smack over the head?

Hurry, hurry, don't give him time to think! I jumped to my feet – I'm small and he was so huge, how could he even hear me if I stayed down there? – and said, 'Sir, Sir! Your Grace, your Majesty! Quince marmalade for you, we all helped make it and the petition is wrong, Sir, wrong, I need to tell you ...'

But he growled. Growled and said, 'Petitions go to Lord Cromwell. Move aside.'

My mother took over. There she was, swinging the

pike away and coming forward, sinking into the deepest of curtsies to the king. Then she stood up, took the box from Ellie, and held it out to the king, saying, 'We have brought you a gift, your Majesty. Quince marmalade. And we are here to beg for mercy. Mercy for my husband, Thomas Wright, accused of treason.'

'And who,' said the king, 'is Thomas Wright?'

'My husband and your faithful servant. Never a traitor, never!'

'And you come here to buy the king's mercy with a box of sweetmeats? Is my mercy so cheap?'

'Not cheap, your Majesty, not cheap! You should have seen how we worked! And each as sweet as the other, the mercy and the quinces. Won't you try a piece and see?' She opened the box and held it up to the king, who seemed to be hesitating between amusement and annoyance. The smallest thing could have tipped him either way.

'Zigzags!' he said, and took one of the red pieces. 'Ha, delicious! Master Cromwell, take the box and offer it to our guests.' The Secretary did so, deadpan. I knew he hated us. And there was all our work disappearing and nothing to show for it. The king was laughing at us, I could see he was.

'Sir!' I cried out desperately, 'Sir, you don't realise, you don't know! The petition is wrong, it doesn't say!'

'You are either a brave child or an ill mannered brat,' said King Harry. 'What does the petition not say?'

'That my father is a good man!' There, I'd said it, got the message out, at last.

'Good men can do wrong things,' said the king.

'Not my father. He's good all through, like oak.' I was so relieved, so glad to have got it said! 'You couldn't know that, Sir, and I wanted to tell you. My father is good. That's all, I'll go now. Thank you for letting me tell you.'

I turned and went away, Ellie close behind me. Ducking under the pike, I looked back, and saw Lippy still out there among all the glittering lords and ladies. What did he think he was doing?

'Lippy,' I called, 'Lippy, come on! Over here!'

CHAPTER SEVENTEEN
LIPPERTY JACK

But Lippy was standing like a statue, gazing into the crowd of French nobles. As I watched, I saw him fling his arms up to heaven, heard him – *heard* him! – utter a scream of joy and then saw him run into the arms of one of the French court ladies. She cried and hugged him, he cried and hugged her, they both talked nineteen to the dozen, *in French*. One of the men standing near them wrapped his arms round the pair of them and burst into tears, kissing them again and again. All the French lords and ladies talked and chattered and shouted and exclaimed. King Harry and all of us watched, interested.

After a while I heard the king say, 'Glad to see each other, aren't they?' and he walked over to the little group. The man, Lippy's father of course, poured out a flood of explanations, some in English and some in French, I thought, but King Harry knows a lot of languages, he could cope. Then Lipperty jumped up and dragged his weeping laughing mother across to us, and she hugged my mother, hugged Ellie, hugged me, and my little silent Lipperty poured out all the things he hadn't said over the past five months. He poured them out in French, but it didn't seem to matter whether we actually understood each other or not.

What it boiled down to – I only gathered some of this later, but never mind – was that Lippy loved boats. One summer's day on a visit to Boulogne he had slipped away from his nurse and gone aboard a boat he liked the look of. He had hidden for fun in a sail-locker, gone to sleep and woken up to find the boat dancing about on the high seas. He had been seasick and frightened, had stayed where he was until the dancing stopped and then had crept ashore, expecting to be punished for being so disobedient and silly. What he didn't realise was that he had left France. He had gone to sleep in Boulogne and woken up off Rye. When he discovered that he couldn't understand anyone, he simply froze with terror. Then I had found him, given him food and saved his life. Saved his life, yes, I probably had.

They had looked and looked for him all over Boulogne, but they never dreamt that by now he wasn't even in the same country.

'Why Lippy?' asked his mother. 'Why do you call him that?'

'Because it's his name,' I said. 'He said that, pointed at himself when he was still there under the breakwater and said "Lipperty Jack". That's who he is, he's my Lipperty Jack. But yours now, of course,' I added hurriedly.

'Lipperty!' said the French lady, still half laughing, half crying. 'He is Le Petit Jacques, little James, that's what we always call him.'

'Oui, c'est ça, le petit Jacques!' said Lipperty. 'Je te l'ai dit, I told you!'

I was glad, of course I was glad, but to have him French, oh no!

'Oh Lippy, Lippy,' I said, 'I don't want you to be French! When I'm a man I'm going to captain one of the king's ships and kill Frenchmen. I don't want to have to kill you, don't be French!' But I knew it was rubbish even as I was saying it.

Just at that moment Bell Harry began to sound, ringing the monks to prayer. This brought me back to reality, and I put my hands together same as always and prayed aloud:

'Lord God, bring my father back!'

Opening my eyes, I saw King Harry looking at me and I explained, 'That's my bell, Bell Harry, it reminds me to pray for my father. I call it mine because we're both Harry. And yours, Sir, now I think of it.'

Lipperty's mother was listening hard to all this. She flung herself on her knees before the king, silks and satins down in the dust, and begged him to save my father as I had saved her son. Her husband came forward to say the same thing, and so did their master, the great French duke King Harry had ridden down from London to meet.

King Harry laughed, waved all three of them away and spoke to me.

'God hears your prayer, boy, and so do I. Your father is free. Master Cromwell, come here!' Up came the Secretary. 'See that this family's petition is fulfilled in every detail. At once.' Lord Cromwell bowed, took the petition from my mother's hands, and went.

Done, settled, finished. All the grand people began to make their way towards Meister Omers, Lippy raced back and gave us all one more hug, then back again to his parents, and all we Canterbury people went home. Our way led us past Saint Peter's, where we turned in, knelt down and gave thanks.

CHAPTER EIGHTEEN
AFTERWARDS

Peter and I rode to Southwark. We'd had to sell Joe, but that was all right, we hired Moonlight, and there was always Cobby. Peter rode Moonlight and Cobby pulled the cart. It's two full days to London, so we stopped overnight in Rochester. Master Secretary had given us a permit, and when we reached the jail we had no trouble getting Father and Uncle Joshua out. Just for a blinding moment I didn't recognise Father – some old man, limping, bloodstained, a straggly white beard – what was this old fool doing leaning on my uncle?

And then it hit me.

And so home.

Peggy Ann came back from Fordwich, full of hugs and kisses and apologies. Johnny and Paul and the others work for the cathedral, of course, not for the Wrights, Father gave them their orders but he wasn't their employer – all the same, they lined up to welcome him and cheered him, the day he was at last fit to start work again. I never saw a bigger smile on anyone's face than I did on Johnny's when Father and Peter and I came in to the cathedral ready for work that morning, and Johnny shouted for three cheers.

We were kept very busy. I began to forget about sailing boats on distant seas and chasing across the Channel to beat up the rotten French. Dear Lippy, for a time I missed him quite badly, but we often got messages and gifts from him and his family, we never forgot each other. He must have done some good listening while he was in England, even if he never spoke – one message from his mother told us that now and then he came out with remarks like, 'For goodness' sake, Harry, where's the plane?' and 'If no one else wants that last bit, I'll have it!' Just imagine, Peter and dreadful Aunt Rose chatting on in the grand courts of France! And I got a message telling me that French kittens are called 'chatons'.

Time did help. Father's left hand came more or less back to normal, but his right hand never recovered its full strength, and he said he thought he would always limp.

Oddly enough we never talked about those bones. It was done, past, and we both knew that. No need to say anything. But once when we were all at table and for some reason Great Aunt Rose was twittering on about a

Wright cousin she hadn't liked and who'd just died and been buried, she said she thought Saint Peter would have no problem deciding where that man ought to go and if he wasn't starting in on a long haul through purgatory, he must have gone straight to the other place, and serve him right. Father stopped with a chicken leg half way to his mouth and said,

'The souls of the righteous are in the hands of God.'

'Oh I daresay!' said Great Aunt, and was going on to ask what reason Father had to suppose Cousin Timothy was righteous, but Father rode right over her and said that God was 'slow to anger and of great kindness'. He took a bite of the chicken, chewed and swallowed it, and went on, 'None of us Wrights is in hell or anywhere near it. Not my father or his father or his father or any of us. Not even in purgatory, got out of there long ago.' He smiled across the table at me, gave an emphatic nod and finished off the piece of chicken. I smiled back at him. My mother smiled too and said, 'Mothers and grandmothers and great grandmothers as well?' and he laughed and said there was no need to ask about them, what could they do but go straight to heaven?

Peter murmured quietly that was no such place as purgatory, but nobody paid any attention and he didn't push it.

My poor uncle seemed to suffer more than my father did. Watching Father walk, sometimes it caught me by surprise and tore at me, the way that strong active man had to ease himself across a room, grabbing at a cupboard top or a table, or in the workshop he would pick up a plane or some other tool and start to use it with his right hand, same as always, and then very soon he'd have to change hands, would battle at working left-handed, and then perhaps he'd have to hand the plane to Peter or even to me, and say, 'You finish it off, will you?' But he kept his mouth tight shut and occasionally managed to smile and I remember him once saying, 'I'm alive, aren't I?' Uncle Josh was less shattered physically, but much more miserable. Mother said perhaps Christmas would cheer him up.

CHAPTER NINETEEN
CHRISTMAS

No, it didn't. We did try ...

The cathedral is glorious and I love every bit of it, but Saint Peter's is home, and Saint Peter's is where we always do the play.

In through the great old arch come the Three Kings, wide awake and talking – they're grumbling about the long journey and the bad-tempered camels, I was one of the camels – on they go to King Herod's palace up near the altar and what a slimy sneaky twister of a king he is! With a red wig, red, is that a safe thing to do, these days? And at first the Kings believe him, they think he really does want to find out where the baby king has been born so that he can go and offer him gifts, and then they curl up and go to sleep and the Archangel Gabriel comes to tell them not to be so stupid, King Herod only wants to kill the baby, and they must go home a different way or little Lord Jesus will die. That was me, Gabriel, I stopped being a camel and got to be the Archangel, tall and important, bringing the message, the Word of God, to the Kings. And all the time the Word of God Himself was lying in a feeding trough on a bed of hay, tiny and helpless (we did think of using Lucy but she wouldn't stay in one place, we had to use a doll). My brother Peter did Joseph, he was very good at putting an arm round Mother Mary and bundling her and the baby off to safety. We had a real donkey. Then Herod came roaring and raging down into the middle of the church with all his soldiers, his 'men of might' like it says in the song, looking for baby boys to kill, yelling and slashing in all directions, and the women cried and screamed – actually that was Father Benedict. He's one of the kindest men I know, but he does enjoy doing Herod! Everyone wept and wailed for a bit and then all the 'dead' infants suddenly appeared in a group together beside the altar, dressed in white and beaming happily, not slaughtered children any more but joyful Holy Innocents. So they're all right.

Uncle Joshua thundered away at the organ and led the choir of angels, he certainly did enjoy that. And how he chivvied those angels! They've never sung so well.

Anne did a very good Mary, bravely protecting her Child from Herod's men. Ellie had decided she didn't want to do it anyway. She did the Innkeeper's Wife and made a very good thing out of it, she was really nasty. Anne's brothers did the Shepherds, and everyone that wasn't a soldier or an angel or anyone else did sheep. Good tuneful sheep they were.

All that happened in the days after Christmas. And then – when the evening's excitement was over and we were thinking of going home, something strange happened. Father Benedict took off his Herod wig and laughed and thanked us and then he reminded us what a holy season this was, not just the glorious coming of the Holy Child but so many saints' days almost all together, we must not forget them. Saint Stephen, he said, and soon Saint John Evangelist, and of course the Holy Innocents – and then he stopped speaking, said nothing for several moments, and still in silence, made the sign of the cross.

After what felt like a long long time, dead silence, no one saying anything, no one hardly *breathing* – he went on, 'And on Old Year's Night there is Saint Sylvester, who chained up the dragon.' Masses would be said in this church and in the Cathedral in honour of all these holy men – and infants – and members of congregations in the city would be welcome at all or any of these services, very welcome.

He had left a huge gap. 29 December is the feast of our saint, Saint Thomas Becket, the holy Archbishop, murdered by a king. Right between Holy Innocents and Saint Sylvester. Nothing said about him, not a word.

Everyone went away in dead silence.

Then Peter muttered a bit about dragons, said there hadn't ever been any such thing. Great Aunt said she wasn't so sure of that. None of us actually spoke the words aloud, 'Saint Thomas.' We were not allowed to honour him, the day was banned, our own saint and we must pretend he didn't exist. 29 December 1170 he had stood up to the king's four knights here in Canterbury in his own cathedral and in this holy place they had drawn their swords and killed him.

King Herod died, didn't he? And it was safe to bring the baby back from Egypt. One day King Harry would ...

And then I could tell Uncle Joshua, Ellie, Father Benedict, everyone. Couldn't I?

A couple of days later he and I were in the stable brushing the dirt out of Cobby's coat.

'I suppose I should go home to Rye,' my uncle said gloomily. 'But I'm not much use here, and I'd be even less there. Just a burden to them.'

'Aren't you going to help teach music at the school?' I asked, squatting down to have a go at the hairy mess round one of Cobby's hind feet.

'Clare suggested that, didn't she? I expect I ought to try.'

'Why don't you?' I said. 'And you needn't stop brushing just because you're miserable, this horse has been rolling, he's disgusting.' Uncle Joshua gave a sort of a laugh and picked up the brush.

'Sorry, I keep forgetting.'

We both worked hard for a bit, and then he slackened off again, leant his head against Cobby's side and said:

'So much destruction. The Priory, the shrine, the Saint's bones burnt, all that – all gone, finished, done with, God's work over a thousand years, destroyed. And your father, the torture – and that part of it was my fault. Mine. If I hadn't wanted to try to save the Saint's bones and got your father involved – and failure, nothing but failure! What a fool I've been.'

'Move over, Uncle Josh, I want to get at his mane.' Cobby shook his head, he was a patient horse but getting tired of this. I combed out some tangles and did some serious thinking. *I knew*, that was the thing, and no one else did, perhaps not even Father for sure. Ought I tell?

I came at it sideways.

'Uncle, Dad's getting better. And he doesn't blame you.'

'No, he's not like that, he wouldn't. I blame myself.'

'Would it be better if you hadn't failed?'

'Hadn't failed? But we did.'

'No, you didn't.'

This horse was never going to get done. My uncle dropped the brush and said, 'Harry, you're not stupid. And you don't usually tease. Do you mean anything?'

I made up my mind.

'Yes,' I said. 'I know where Saint Thomas's bones are and they aren't burnt and he hasn't left his cathedral. And don't you dare say a word about this to anyone in the whole world. Ever.'

I put the comb and brushes back on the shelf, patted long-suffering Cobby, left the stable and went to wash for dinner.

AUTHOR'S NOTE

In this story King Henry VIII is so to speak between wives. He has had three, and will have three more. He really was very tall, six foot two, or even three, inches and by now enormously fat, and did have red hair. His only legitimate son, little Prince Edward, became king when Henry died in 1547, but he was never strong and died when he was fifteen.

Changes in the way people were allowed or ordered to worship God in England came in bit by bit. At the time of the story in the summer of 1538, it was thought very wrong to read the Bible in anything but Latin, you could be burnt alive as a heretic if you weren't careful, but later the same year it was decreed that an English Bible must be placed in every church. It was still thought dangerous to have one in your own home, where all sorts of people, even women! might read it and get silly ideas.

The Wright family and their friends and relatives are all invented, and so are Lipperty Jack and his parents. The king, Prior Goldwell and Secretary Thomas Cromwell were all real. The Prior hoped to become dean of the cathedral under the new system, but didn't get the job, he had to retire, with a pension. Thomas Cromwell arranged a fourth marriage for the king, but the lady, Anne of Cleves, was so unattractive and smelt so bad, Henry detested her and sent her away. He had Thomas Cromwell executed in 1540. (People get the Cromwells mixed up, but it was a distant relative of his, Oliver, who became Lord Protector of England in 1653.)

We don't know whether anyone really did try to save Thomas Becket's bones from the king's men. Bits of the cathedral are dug up now and then but nothing has ever been found.

Also by Jan Shirley published by Ragged Bears Publishing

THE ROAD TO STONEHENGE

'Why do they keep wanting to kill me?
How can I make them stop?'

Young Krenn lives in the West Country. Her name means 'doesn't belong' and true enough, she was found abandoned as a baby. Now the time has come for the tribe who adopted her to send her away, eastwards where the great temples are, to find her own people. It will be a long, hard journey and she must travel alone.

Will Krenn find her true family? And will they like each other?

An engaging tale of a girl's search for the truth set against the meeting between an old and a new world.

'A powerful book that holds the attention and entertains. The reader is swept along, lost in it all'
Michael Morpurgo

'A hard journey for Krenn and a big adventure ... a great book to read because as soon as you start reading you can't stop'
Nine-year-old reader

The Road to Stonehenge

We owe her nothing. Seven years' care, eight, she owes us. She ought to go away from us as naked as we found her!' It was Ensy speaking, Old Woman of the tribe, priestess. 'But of course we shan't do that. I've given her warm clothing, and food for six days. It's all we can spare.'

'She can travel with us to begin with, surely,' said Hoony. He had obeyed his own mother when she was Old Woman and he was going to obey Ensy, but it wouldn't be easy. He could remember her as a bossy little girl and then as a nagging wife–one of Haldo's thanks be! not his–and he wished very much that the Stone hadn't had to go to her. 'She can travel with us to begin with,' he repeated.

'No. We are to go south, the Old Woman said so, and Krenn is to go and find this temple of hers. There's nothing like that to the south of us, she'll have to go east. That's where the great temples are.'

Hoony and his people were busy packing up for the move. There was no time to lose, it was already well into autumn and the seed should have been in the ground by now. Most of them would much rather have stayed where they were and got on with the planting and risked a bad winter and worn-out soil, but the goddess had to be right. If She says go, you go.

But they would have to hurry. Even if they only went down river along the Barle to the land they'd left a dozen years ago-it should have recovered by now-it would take them several days. Goats can be made to move quite fast, cows are not too bad, but pigs are the most contrary beasts the Lady ever made. Then when they arrived and had put up houses and a fence to keep the stock in and the wolves out, they must start the autumn slaughtering and preserving, not to mention clearing the ground and getting next year's crops planted. What they'd have to do now was send an advance party to start putting up shelters. Was it worth taking the rooftrees with them, or should they cut fresh when they got there? Hoony had a thousand and one things on his mind; he hadn't the time to quarrel with Ensy over Krenn. Besides, Ensy spoke for the Lady, and that was that.

'Krenn, Krenn, where are you?' he called. 'Ah, there you are. Ens–the Old Woman's right, you go east. Flint-traders and other people, they come from that way, and I've heard some of them talking about the great temples they have over there. Much bigger than any of ours, so they say. But they're a long way off, you'll have to keep on and on. Keep going towards the sun as it rises, and the holy Mother go with you.' He slung a short deerskin cloak off his shoulders and put it round hers. 'My mother dressed these skins for me-wear it for me and for her.' He kissed her, and turned away to get on with taking down the roof-trees.

Ensy flushed an angry red and began to mutter something about wicked wastefulness but Hoony stared her down and she was quiet.

Young Jinsy came rushing up. He had loved Krenn all his life and he was furious.

'I'm going with her!' he shouted. 'You're wicked, wicked and cruel! How can you send her out all alone like that, when she's lived with us ever since she was born?'

Krenn herself looked at him in horror. That anyone should speak like that about an order of the Old Woman, of the goddess! She wouldn't have been surprised to see him struck by lightning.

What did strike him, and hard, was his mother's fist. Delighted to be able to relieve her feelings and do right at the same time, Ensy dealt him a hearty clip on the side of the head and knocked him flying. No one took very much notice. Krenn looked to where he curled up in the lee of one of the houses, rubbing his head-yes, he was all right. She nodded goodbye to all her non-relatives, picked up her bundle and went away.

All this happened because once upon a time, around five thousand years ago, a tiny new-born baby girl had been found in thick woodland, found and rescued. Now she was seven, going on eight.

'Tell me again, Nanna,' she would say to the old woman who loved her, 'tell me about when I was found in the forest.' And the old woman would tell her all over again about the time Hoony's people were travelling through the forest and how one day they came to a place where other people had camped before them and they thought they could hear a child crying.

'And that was me, Nanna, that was me!'

'Yes, that was you. They'd put you out to die, but you'd been well wrapped up in a fine piece of stuff, not leather, very soft, it was like nothing we'd ever seen— someone loved you all right, and there you were alive and yelling. You weren't going to die, not you! And the men said, "Don't look for it, leave it, it can't be healthy, wouldn't have been put out if it was all right," but my own daughter's baby had just died, she still had the milk in her breasts and it was hurting her because there wasn't any baby to take it away. So she said, "Find it, find it, give it to me!" and I looked among the trees and under the bushes and there you were, bawling with rage! And I unwrapped you and looked at you and you were a fine girl child, no mark or damage of any kind, and I gave you to my own girl to suckle. How she cried out with relief as you began to take the milk from her, poor girl!'

'Had I been there long, Nanna? Why didn't a wolf take me? Or a bear?'

'Long enough! We found the ashes of their fire, those strangers, whoever they were, and they were three or four days old. And the wolves and the bears–well, either they weren't feeling very hungry, or the Great Mother protected you! I was quite sure She'd saved you to be a blessing to my own girl, and so I wouldn't let the men kill you or leave you behind. I'm the one who says who lives and who dies in this family, they know that!'

'Well yes, I should think so,' said Krenn. Hoony was Old Man of the family but it was the women, especially the Old Woman, Hoony's mother, who mattered. They made all the decisions. When it was time for the family to shift to a new district, which of the newborn babies were to be kept and which put out to die, which sick people would get better and ought to be helped and which ones put out in the woods to go to the goddess–all that sort of thing.

'I should think so! But then she went and died herself.'

'Not for a long time,' said the Old Woman, smiling at Krenn, 'not till after your naming. You remember her, don't you?'

'Of course I do, very well. I loved her a lot. But, Nanna, I wish you hadn't let them call me Krenn, 'doesn't belong', I don't like it. Why did you?'

'Because it was true. You don't belong to our family, or to any of the families that use the forest. They were strangers passing through, those people who left you, they were krenn. Even the stuff you were wrapped in, we've never used anything like that, never seen such a thing. It's no use pretending.'

'Three whole years,' said Krenn, 'you'd think they'd have forgotten I was *krenn* by that time.' Children in this family were not given names until they had stayed alive for at least three years and you could be fairly sure you were not going to lose them. The names all had meanings–Hoony was 'strong right hand', young Jinsy was 'jumps first, thinks later', Krenn was 'not one of ours'. 'Nanna' was only a nickname–the true name of the Old Woman, like the Name of the goddess, the Great Mother, the Lady, was never spoken.